CITY OF DAEVAS

BOOK 3 OF THE BAKA DJINN CHRONICLES

J F MEHENTEE

1

Roshan exited the crumbling, sand-filled city through a space once occupied by doors. She didn't have to look back. The djinn, silent except for their footsteps, followed and fanned out behind her after clearing the city's west-facing wall. Five hundred pairs of eyes, their irises surrounded by red flames, watched her. She was ready and so were they.

The rising sun cleared the city and lit the black line of approaching guardsmen. The sky, however, remained blue-grey.

Roshan blinked, and the approaching dark blur resolved into a column of cavalrymen, their numbers stretching back towards the horizon. At their centre rode a figure dressed in white, his mount matching the colour of his magus robes. The high magus raised an arm. The column of mounted guardsmen halted. Guardsmen on foot burst from between their ranks and swarmed past them to form two rows of archers, the front kneeling and the back standing. As one, they nocked their arrows.

Roshan raised her arms. The back of her hands had turned the same colour as the sky. Lines of orange flame whirled beneath her skin.

'Don't do this,' a voice said. 'This is not the way.'

The archers launched their arrows.

Burn, Roshan thought.

The arrows burst into an orange line of flame and hung in the air as if a cloud. The flaming veil boiled and swelled for three heartbeats, its light brighter than the sun's, and then it contracted. Jagged thunderbolts of orange spewed from it, each bolt lancing an archer. The bowmen erupted so quickly, there wasn't time to cry out. No sooner had the cloud of flame above exhausted itself than the row of burning archers shrank before discharging more flaming bolts, this time at the soldiers behind them.

Roshan observed how her thought worked its way through the high magus's army, reducing it to a trailing column of soot and ash.

'What do you feel?' the voice said.

She recognised it now and knew that she lay in a tent outside Baka, dreaming.

'Nothing. I'm not sorry for what I did, if that's what you mean. I did what needed doing to save the djinn.'

She heard nothing until Manah sighed.

'Turn around,' he said.

She knew then she'd erred. She tried to wake up but couldn't.

Roshan turned. So that she didn't have to take in the full extent of her mistake, she squinted.

Like High Magus Sassan and his army, she had reduced the djinn to a black line that stretched the length of the city's west wall.

A winged bull with a bearded human head, Manah, stood at her side.

'You will have to choose between restoring the daevas' auric energy and confronting the high magus. All it takes is a thought and your aura will touch all the djinn and daevas. As you channel your energy to them, you'll bind yourself to them.'

Roshan surveyed the djinn's remains. The desert wind blew across it, scattering the djinn's ashes and erasing the black line.

'So, if I were to help the daevas, help them become djinn again, I'd hurt them if I fought Sassan at the same time.'

Manah nodded.

'Until you can master sabaoth magic, I'm afraid so. You must do one or the other, but you're not ready to do both.'

Roshan wanted to fight, and she wanted to rescue Yesfir.

'There's around four hundred daevas and one hundred djinn, most of them camped outside Baka. How long could I channel energy to so many?'

As if she'd asked the wrong question, Manah shook his head.

'As I explained earlier, Domain power will replenish the energy you pass on, leaving you filled with sabaoth energy. You'll feel drained, and you'll need time to recover your strength, but that's all.'

If she knew how long it took to regain her strength, perhaps between breaks from channelling energy, she could help with the fighting and Yesfir's rescue. Before she could ask him, Manah began to fade.

'Is Yesfir all right?' she asked instead.

'She is,' Manah's shadow said. 'But it won't be long before she submits completely to the seal's influence.'

Roshan woke and found herself back inside the tent. Navid lay next to her. So as not to wake her brother, she rose quietly. After shape-shifting three times and getting injured, he needed his rest.

She'd reached the tent flap when he spoke.

'Where are you going?'

Roshan looked back and saw Navid awake and sitting up. She told him about her dream and Manah's news.

'I have to tell the prince,' she said, 'and Behrouz needs to know what's happening to Yesfir.'

Navid pushed himself up and onto his feet.

'I'm coming with you. If there's a plan to rescue Yesfir, I want to be part of it.'

Roshan winced at the mention of a rescue plan. If she hadn't hesitated, if she'd killed the high magus instead, a rescue wouldn't be necessary.

Outside, Roshan glanced up. From the sun's position, it would be another two hours before noon.

Four hundred paces separated their tent from the city. Even from that distance, the amount of work required to make the city defendable was plain. Baka lacked doors, the west-facing wall contained a breach and sand covered most of the northern watchtower.

Things weren't any better inside.

'Look,' Navid said, sounding aghast.

On their left they saw sand covering the watchtower being shovelled into bags. Daevas carried the bags out of the city to empty them.

'At the rate they're going, the city won't be defensible for years,' he said.

If daevas hefting bags filled with sand was the only way to conserve what remained of the djinn's auric energy, Baka was in more trouble than she'd imagined. If Yesfir and the daevas weren't being held prisoner, she'd raise a portal to Arshak and level the encampment, solving the problem in a single swoop. She'd do it and live with the guilt of all those deaths. The thought of having to face Behrouz and share news about Yesfir filled her with dread.

'Over half, maybe three-quarters of the buildings are uninhabitable,' Navid said.

His comment interrupted her thoughts and yanked her out of herself. Somehow, while she'd mulled over Yesfir and the captured daevas, they'd ventured farther into the city and now approached the ziggurat at its centre.

'No wonder everyone's having to live in tents,' Navid

continued. 'What was the king thinking when he sent everyone here?'

There was no point reminding Navid that, by now, the king had hoped he'd have Solomon's seal. Then, there'd be no need to conserve auric energy. Her brother's question, however, was still valid. There had to be other cities the king could have chosen, or —if he had the seal—built one like Iram from the foundations up. What was so important about this long-abandoned city?

Navid spotted the prince sitting on the ziggurat's steps. He sat with rounded shoulders and his face lined. A deep, visible crack snaked its way from the base of the structure and stopped two-thirds of the way up. A strong gust might collapse the building and send it crashing down on him.

The prince spotted them, stood and waved.

'Well, he looks happy to see us,' Navid whispered. He waved back as they continued on.

They climbed the steps, Roshan ready to hare down them at the slightest breeze.

'Welcome to Baka,' the prince said. One corner of his mouth turned down. 'Right now, it isn't much.' He gestured for them to sit, the step wide enough for them all to take a seat.

Untroubled by the ziggurat's soundness, Navid sat down first. Roshan was about to say she was more comfortable standing, but her brother scowled at her.

'Manah visited Roshan again,' Navid said.

Grateful for her brother's directness, Roshan described Yesfir's well-being. The prince shrank at the news and blood left his face.

'Did Manah say how long before my poor niece breaks?'

Too wrapped up in her choice between channelling her auric energy and fighting, she hadn't asked.

'I'm sorry, I don't know, Your Highness.'

The prince grimaced.

'Let's make one thing clear, both of you,' he said. 'We're no longer in Iram. Out here, I'm Emad—not Your Highness and not Prince Emad, just *Emad*.'

Navid nodded.

Hadn't her brother found that strange, the prince—Emad— insisting on such a thing, especially with Yesfir being tortured and the threat of an invasion looming?

'From now on, it's just Emad,' Navid said. He nudged Roshan between the ribs.

'Yes,' she said, nodding. 'Of course.'

The prince clenched his right hand over his left and squeezed.

'If Yesfir's close to breaking, Sassan and his soldiers will soon appear outside Baka. Then we're finished.'

The weight of her news made the prince crumple.

'Manah told me how to channel my auric energy to *all* the djinn and daevas. If everyone could weave magic, we could transform this city in a matter of days instead of years.'

The prince stared at her as if the burden he carried had gotten heavier.

'And what about you? There are five hundred of us here. You can't possibly have enough auric energy to go around.'

Roshan didn't know whether to be grateful or worried that he'd put her own welfare before everyone else's. She shook her head.

'You mustn't worry. Domain power, the power sabaoth use to weave magic, will replenish it. Depending on what's going on, I'll get tired and nothing more.'

The prince's gaze never left her.

'Are you sure? You're not just saying that to help, or because you're feeling guilty about the prisoners in Arshak?'

Roshan's face reddened, and she glanced down.

'You're right; I feel terrible about what happened there. But that's not the reason I want to help. I want the high magus to stop what he's doing to the djinn and daevas. If I can help them regain their powers, even temporarily, they'll stand a chance. I'm offering more than shovelling sand into bags and carrying them out of a city with no doors.'

The passion behind her answer surprised her.

The prince smiled. He straightened, and his demeanour softened.

'What happened in Arshak to those daevas in the alley, the little boy, isn't your fault. And it's the same with what happened last night. The fault lies with that deluded high magus. He has to be stopped. With so few of us left, we have to find a way to make do while suffering minimal loses or, ideally, none.' He glanced around at his surroundings.

'My brother insists Baka is our new home. Until I can convince him otherwise, our first priority is to make the city both habitable and defendable. Our second is to rescue Yesfir. If you believe channelling your energy won't harm you, then we need your help right away.'

Roshan couldn't tell what it was about the way he looked at her. She'd seen something similar cross Yesfir's face. It happened whenever she got a recitation right for the first time. The prince was proud of her. And there was something more than just pride. Roshan couldn't be sure, because she'd only seen it directed at others. He looked as if he believed in her.

Roshan sat up.

'I can channel energy to everyone right now,' she said.

2

E mad watched as the daevas filed into the square in front of the ziggurat. The djinn soon followed, although they must have taken a different route, because they entered the square from a side street. Just as they'd pitched their tents at a distance from the daevas', so the djinn stood in the square, a gap of ten paces separating them. The djinn and daevas standing either side of the gap acknowledged those they knew with a nod or a wave. Emad smiled when he saw a djinn child pointing excitedly at his daeva grandparents. For a moment, he put aside his concerns for Yesfir and studied the crowd. He saw among their faces exhaustion, fear and—from those watching him and Roshan standing on the ziggurat's steps—anticipation.

He raised his hand for silence.

'Are you ready?' he said to Roshan, from the side of his mouth. The girl pushed her shoulders back and nodded. 'Good luck,' he whispered. *I hope this works,* he thought. Emad lowered his hand. 'From this day forward,' he said, addressing the square, 'there will be no daevas, only djinn.'

He held his breath and scanned the larger group, the daevas.

Looks of puzzlement met his statement. Then a hubbub

started among the daevas but also developed among a group of djinn who spotted a change in the colour of the flames surrounding their neighbour's irises. Parents stared at their children with an intensity that made them either laugh or cry. Couples hugged. The gap between the djinn and daevas shrank, until Iram's djinn roamed the square, searching for friends and family.

He glanced at Roshan. She appeared unaffected by her channelling to so many. Emad smiled at her. With her full attention focussed on Behrouz and Zana, she hadn't noticed it. Aware that so much needed doing before dusk, he held up his hand again. Apart from the odd child still crying, a hush filled the square.

He thanked Roshan and then explained to the gathering the limitations of her gift.

'Your auric energy will need replenishing, so this isn't a permanent fix. If you take off your bracelet, you will break the connection between you and Roshan, and you'll no longer receive her energy. We are five hundred and Roshan is only one. To avoid overburdening her, we will work in shifts. When you're not working, please refrain from using magic unnecessarily.'

He paused, studied the crowd's faces to ensure they had heard and understood what he'd said.

Now comes the bad news.

'As you all know, the high magus has Solomon's seal. His attack on Iram means an attack on Baka is likely and soon. We must prepare the city for this, and we must work fast. I've assembled a restoration team. They will assign you tasks and the time of day during which you must complete them.

'For Baka to remain our home, it must be defendable. Those are our priorities for today. Members of the defences team, the engineering team and the supplies teams will meet every other hour to assess the progress being made. If we are falling behind in one area, they might ask you to stop what you're doing and join a different group. Please be flexible. Even with magic, we have so much to achieve before the light fades.' He paused to let what he'd said sink in. 'Work begins within the hour. Thank you for coming and thank you, once again, Roshan.'

The djinn turned and emptied the square faster than they had filled it. They strode away with purposeful and confident steps.

He turned to Roshan, followed her gaze and saw how Behrouz, Zana and Navid had remained behind. Emad descended the steps and approached them, Roshan close behind.

Behrouz clutched his upper arms. Zana lacked his normal cheerfulness, dark crescents under his eyes.

'Roshan told me about what's happening to Yesfir,' Behrouz said. 'We have to send a rescue party to Arshak before she starts raising portals.'

Emad cringed at the memory of the daeva he'd beheaded outside Iram. It left him with little doubt that, once he had the coordinates, Sassan would use Yesfir to transport his army here.

'Give me an hour, Behrouz. I need to make sure work gets started. Then I'll go to Iram and speak to Fiqitush. I'm sure he's already come up with a plan.'

Behrouz's jaw muscles bunched. This wasn't the answer he wanted.

'Every hour is an hour she's being tortured by the seal.' He touched his bracelet. 'She's weakening—I can feel it.'

As a captain, Emad had dealt with similar behaviour. After they'd docked and disembarked, and whenever a crewman got into trouble, he was always the one having to stop the rest of the crew from rushing off to help them. He'd have to keep everyone calm before the situation grew out of hand and out of proportion. It didn't make him popular.

'*We* will get her back, Behrouz. If you try to rescue her yourself, and you get captured, you'll only add to the problem: Sassan will have a second djinni to raise portals for him.' He wanted to remind Behrouz that Yesfir was his niece and Fiqitush was her father; he wasn't the only one who worried about her and wanted her back. Behrouz, however, didn't deserve to be patronised. 'Be patient. While you wait, help prepare the city's defences. We can't afford to do anything that will put Baka in further danger.'

Behrouz's expression soured.

'Two hours,' he said, his voice a growl. 'If you don't have a plan, I'll go to Arshak on my own. All I care about is my wife.'

Behrouz turned and marched away, Zana beside him. Navid stayed behind.

'There has to be something we can do?' he said.

Emad sighed, then shook his head.

'If I were in that djinni's boots, I wouldn't wait two hours. It wouldn't even matter if I failed, because I wouldn't be able to live with myself if I didn't try. Thankfully, Behrouz is more disciplined than I am. It won't last much longer, though. We'll have to do something.'

Roshan chewed her lip.

'Like what?'

Take away his bracelet so he isn't a danger to himself and all of us.

'I don't know,' Emad said. 'If you have any ideas, I'd gladly hear them. Otherwise, let's see what Fiqitush comes up with.'

The twins gazed everywhere but at him.

'Don't worry,' he said. 'I can't think of anything either.'

Fiqitush was better at this kind of thing. Emad would return to Iram in an hour. As he saw it, his first priority wasn't to rescue Yesfir. He needed to break the bond between his brother and Iram so Fiqitush could enter Baka.

3

Sassan opened his eyes. The light penetrating the canvas above suggested he'd slept for only an hour. Although the poppy juice helped calm the pain, he remained groggy and in need of more sleep.

He rubbed his face. The seal's band touched his cheek. The djinni, Yesfir, looked as exhausted as he felt. The memory of her struggling against the seal got him out of bed. She was the only good thing to have happened after last night's disaster.

Afacan was furious at the loss of all twelve of his men and Tamraz's escape. The sudden severing of the connection between him and the daeva made Sassan doubt Tamraz had escaped. More likely, he'd been killed before he could return to Arshak. That theory had done little to appease the general.

Sassan splashed water on his face. He reached for a towel and saw the tablet next to it on his table. How many times had he read it this morning? He had followed the instructions, God's instructions, to the wedge-shaped mark. So, why had he failed? The continuous pain from helping Tamraz raise three portals and the frequent doses of poppy juice muddied his thoughts.

Sassan pulled on his tunic. Either he'd done something wrong or God continued to test him.

Test or no test, I need results, he thought to himself, *otherwise, I'll lose the general's trust and then the emperor's trust.*

Sassan grabbed the golden arrow and exited his tent.

He slunk through the encampment and hoped he wouldn't run into Afacan. News about what had happened in Iram must have spread, because Sassan heard the murmur of voices in his wake. Each guardsman he encountered stood to attention as he passed, but he felt their eyes on his back.

Convinced the encampment doubted he fully controlled this expedition, he reached the tent without incident.

Yesfir sat slumped in a chair, her tunic crumpled and stained. Sassan ordered the guard to remove her manacles.

'And pull up the sleeves of her tunic,' he said.

Yesfir raised her head. The guard removed the manacles from around her ankles, and the flames surrounding her irises brightened. Her eyes widened and then her brow furrowed when she saw Sassan. She returned his stare. Sassan smiled. She'd tried to hide it behind defiance, but Sassan had caught the quiver of her lower lip.

He waited until the guard had removed both pairs of manacles. They lay in front of her, making it impossible for Yesfir to stand and to close the gap between them.

She is strong, but God is stronger, and I am His instrument.

This would be their fourth hour together, and he'd make certain it would be the last before she broke and surrendered to the seal.

'Yesfir,' he said, 'please tell me where Baka is.'

Her eyes turned to slits.

'I don't know where it is.'

He positioned himself in front of the manacles and pushed one towards her with the side of his foot. He held out the seal and asked her again.

She gasped. Her head drooped forward, and she shook it.

'I don't know.'

Sassan braced himself and then touched his aura to Yesfir's. The seal's power flowed through his body and into hers.

Pain, he thought.

Yesfir flung her head back and screamed.

Sassan curled his hands into fists as the muscles in his forearms liquified. All that stopped him from crying out was the line of wheals that appeared down both of Yesfir's forearms. He gritted his teeth as the red welts swelled and filled with fluid.

'Tell me where Baka is.'

Yesfir screamed again. The blisters burst. Blood and clear fluid spilled onto her tunic and leggings.

The pain caused Sassan to drop onto one knee. He was within reach of her. She could grab him, recite an incantation. Instead, she wept.

'I asked you a question, Yesfir.'

He squeezed the arrow's shaft in anticipation. The second transfer of the seal's energy lasted a heartbeat. It blurred Sassan's vision and threatened to choke him. He blinked tears back. Yesfir howled. The sound hid Sassan's own gasps for breath.

Blood seeped from under the djinni's fingernails.

Sassan swallowed.

'Look, Yesfir,' he said, sounding as if he were talking to a child.

Heal, he thought.

He touched her right forearm with the arrow's tip. A waft of cool air touched Sassan's face and left him feeling more solid. Yesfir's forearm had healed. The blood on her right hand had turned to a red powder.

'Behold God's work. He will take away all your pain. God needs your help, Yesfir. Help Him and you will never suffer again. Just tell me where Baka is.'

A tear hung from the tip of Yesfir's nose. The rate her chest rose and fell began to slow.

Sassan saw her blink several times and then avoid his gaze. She shut her eyes, sending more tears spilling from them. Her lips parted.

I've broken her.

The djinni's lips closed and became a thin line. She opened her eyes, a hardness blazing behind them. He stood before she could shake her head. He tapped her left forearm, just above her silver bracelet, and cleared it of wounds.

Sassan gave a weary sigh and turned. He needed to calm himself; otherwise, this mulish djinni would end up like Pudil: a pillar of flame.

Sassan caught the guardsman staring at him. He'd seen a similar expression on the general's face. The guardsman didn't approve of him torturing a woman.

'What's your name?'

The guardsman stood to attention, his eyes bulging.

'Iskhaq, High Magus.'

The burning in Sassan's forearms had eased at the same time Yesfir's skin and nail beds had returned to normal. Its release had left him dizzy and saddened.

'I never thought bringing the One Religion to the daevas would involve torture. This is God's work, but I find it abhorrent. Do you think it's a sin that I, the High Magus, should feel that way about my work? Am I a sinner, Iskhaq?'

The guardsman's eyes darted around as though the answer to the high magus's question lay somewhere inside the tent.

Iskhaq stuttered, looking desperate to fill the silence.

Sassan walked over to the guardsman. He had to stand on tiptoes to place a calming hand on Iskhaq's shoulder.

'I shouldn't have asked such a thing. It was a moment of weakness, and it was unfair to burden you in such a way. Be calm.' He removed his hand, only half-turned and then stopped. 'Iskhaq,' he said over his shoulder. 'Might I ask a favour of you?'

The guardsman raised his eyebrows.

'Of course, High Magus.'

Sassan nodded his thanks.

'Tonight, during prayers, will you pray for me and ask God to forgive me my sin?'

Iskhaq scanned the floor, his eyes blinking. He rubbed his brow as though it itched.

'I—I will, High Magus,' the guardsman stammered.

Sassan groaned his relief and smiled.

'Good man,' he said, with a nod. He cleared his throat. 'Right, Iskhaq, God isn't done with this...'

Yesfir sat upright and stared ahead, her eyes dry.

Sassan recognised that look: he'd seen it on Tamraz's face.

'Yesfir,' he said. She raised her head. The red flames around her irises continued to burn, but her gaze lacked depth. Sassan gripped the arrow, curbing his excitement. 'Yesfir, are you ready to talk?'

Without a pause and with the same vacant expression, Yesfir nodded.

4

F ine particles of sand rained down from the roof of Iram's cavern. Emad had to cover his nose and mouth to stop himself from inhaling them. An eerie silence filled the city, its main road and buildings still and empty. Unsure where his brother might be, Emad entered the palace and made his way to Fiqitush's chambers. A mustiness pervaded the corridors. He'd noticed the dampness as soon as he'd arrived four days earlier, but he didn't remember it smelling this strong—not ten hours previously, when he was last there. And it wasn't just the smell. Something else felt wrong about the deserted city.

He found the door to the chambers ajar. Emad saw no point in knocking.

His brother lay on his bed, his eyes closed. Shephatiah knelt by him. The djinni dabbed Fiqitush's brow with a moist cloth before dipping it into a bowl to wet it again. A quip, about the djinni overdoing his commitment to duty, lodged in Emad's throat. His brother's skin had turned pasty, and he struggled to breathe.

'Fiqitush?'

His brother's eyelids fluttered open. Fiqitush smiled at Emad and then turned his attention to Shephatiah. He patted the djinni's hand.

'He's here now. It's time to go.' Fiqitush's face puckered as he pushed himself up. He leaned forward and kissed Shephatiah on the forehead. 'Thank you for everything you've done.'

Shephatiah rose and bowed deeply. The djinni passed Emad and bowed again, his eyes teary.

Emad wasn't sure what he'd witnessed.

Fiqitush patted the mattress, indicating Emad should join him.

'What's happened to you?' Emad said.

Beside the bed lay a boxed tablet and a rag soaked in blood. Fiqitush snatched up the rag and coughed into it.

'When I destroyed part of the city, I destroyed a part of me.' He tapped his chest. 'I told you; Iram and I are inextricably linked.'

Emad stood.

'I'll get Roshan. She'll make you better. And while she's at it, I'll get her to unbind you from this place.'

Fiqitush shook his head. He patted the mattress again.

'The magic holding this place together and keeping me alive is almost gone. Time has run out.'

Emad sat next to his brother.

'So, you're going to just lie here and die? What about Yesfir? She's still in Arshak. Sassan has her, remember.'

Fiqitush reached across and clamped his hand around Emad's.

'Save her, but only if it doesn't risk other djinn being captured. Yesfir left Iram to teach Roshan djinn magic. She made a sacrifice then, and my daughter will make it again if it prevents others from being caught.'

Emad tensed and hoped it wouldn't come to that.

His hand still gripped around Emad's, Fiqitush rolled forward to reach the boxed tablet on the floor. He let go of Emad's hand and placed the box on his brother's lap.

'The tablet inside contains everything I know about Baka and my plans for it.'

The city's a wreck. What else is there to know about it?

Fiqitush rolled his eyes.

'Don't look like that, brother. Don't judge things with only your eyes.'

Emad picked up the box. It and the tablet were light, but Fiqitush had passed him a weighty responsibility.

'What am I supposed to do with this?' he said. Emad despised himself for asking. Fiqitush could never leave Iram, and there was nothing he, his brother, could do about it.

'Baka wasn't built in its present location.' Fiqitush wagged a finger before Emad could interrupt. 'If you don't believe me, dig away some sand beneath one of the city's walls. Examine the city's foundations.' The pitch of Fiqitush's voice rose. His excitement triggered a coughing fit. He held up a hand and wiped the rag over his mouth with the other. His breathing still laboured, he continued. 'Baka isn't just rock and mortar. It's *alive*.'

Emad wanted to stop his brother, ignore the madness he spouted and get him to Baka. Once he was better, he'd do whatever Fiqitush asked—even if it meant digging beneath a wall with his bare hands.

'It's alive, I tell you. Two of the city's three wells are dry because the city is sleeping. Check for yourself. An aquifer doesn't feed the only functioning well. Ancient magic feeds water from who knows where into it. Once you've woken the city, the two wells—' Fiqitush screwed his eyes shut and shook his head. 'None of that's important. All you need to know for now is that once it awakens, magic will lift Baka into the air, and the entire city—buildings, people, wells, everything within its walls—can pass through a portal.'

Emad considered his brother's words. If Fiqitush were right, there'd be no need to confront the high magus and his army. They could disappear.

'How do we wake the city?'

Fiqitush coughed again. With each fit, he withered more. His brother patted the box with its tablet inside.

'Before you were born, Grandmother told me stories about a flying city. This tablet contains those stories.' He grimaced. 'I found nothing about how to wake it. I'm afraid that's something you must discover with the others.' Fiqitush gripped Emad's shoulder. 'Help me up,' he said. 'Then raise a portal to the tunnel leading up to the desert.'

Emad tucked the box under one arm, helped Fiqitush up and raised a portal.

His brother chuckled.

'I love you, Emad. You don't like giving up—do you?'

The destination window opened onto Baka.

Fiqitush shuffled towards the portal. The boarding window flickered, and the portal collapsed.

'Iram and I are the same. For me to enter that portal, you'd have to slot the city through it, too.' He nudged Emad. 'Don't say I didn't warn you.'

Emad raised a portal. A few remaining firestones glowed in the tunnel's alcoves. They stepped through it together.

'It's been decades since I felt sand between my toes and the sun on my face,' Fiqitush said.

They walked the short distance to the entrance, Emad's hips aching from having to match his brother's narrow gait. Fiqitush rested his arm on Emad's shoulder. The weight leaning on him became lighter with each step.

'What's wrong?' Fiqitush said. 'Why are you looking at me that way?'

Emad's throat constricted.

'You're looking older,' he said. 'Your skin's gone grey. We should go back.' He stopped walking. 'Roshan can channel some of her energy into you. You'll get better, Iram will get better and you can run things from here until we find a way for you to leave.'

Behind and below them, as if in protest, the city rumbled. The tunnel shook.

Fiqitush glanced behind them. Emad looked back to see a cloud of dust.

'It's too late for that, Emad.' Fiqitush pointed at the entrance farther ahead. 'Come on.'

Emad wanted to yell at the city to release his brother.

A bout of coughing stalled them.

Once they were walking again, Fiqitush said, 'Promise me three things.'

Emad stared straight ahead and swallowed.

'That depends.'

Fiqitush's breathing crackled.

'You used to say that when we were boys.' Fiqitush nodded once. 'All right, then. The first thing I want you to promise me is that you'll take care of the djinn and daevas. They need you and they need a leader.' He cleared his throat. 'Second, promise me you'll save Yesfir, so long as you don't put Baka in danger. And after you've saved her, tell her how proud I am of her and how much I love her.'

Emad bit his lower lip and gave a vigorous nod.

'You haven't heard your third promise yet, brother.' Fiqitush staggered, and his legs collapsed beneath him.

Emad caught him.

Behind them, dust had moved farther up the tunnel.

Emad shoved the box and its tablet into his tunic. He slid a hand under Fiqitush's knees and stood, holding his brother, who weighed no more than a babe.

'The third promise'—Fiqitush's breath and voice had become a hiss—'is that you tell the twins you're their father. Let them decide what to do about that.'

They reached the entrance and stepped out under the noonday sun.

'Promise, Emad?' his brother whispered.

Emad's voice croaked.

'Yes, I will, Fiqitush.'

The ground shuddered. Emad thought he heard rain. Still carrying Fiqitush, he saw how a crevice had formed. He had heard sand pouring into the cavern below.

Emad looked down to see his brother's cheek pressed against his tunic. He looked as if he'd fallen asleep.

The ground shook again. Emad found his arms and shoulders ached and his knees began to fold. With each passing moment, his brother grew heavier.

Iram wants him back.

Emad bent down on one knee. With a reluctance that made him choke, he lay his brother on the ground. Sand slipped past his boots. If he remained there any longer, he'd get sucked into the cavern.

He leaned forward, kissed Fiqitush on both cheeks and let go.

5

Zana's head ached, but not from the heat of the noonday sun. After their encounter with Uncle Emad, Father had sat down on the ziggurat's steps, his foot and fingers tapping while he waited for Uncle's return. With his jaw muscles flexed, Father had worn a constant scowl. Zana had thought it best to leave him alone.

So, for the past hour, Zana had wandered the city and hoped to bump into Nahrian. At first, he'd just wanted to tell her about Mother but, venturing deeper into the city, he'd realised this was the perfect time for Ramina to teach him how to shape-shift. The only way for him to help Father rescue Mother was if he were humanoid. As a manticore, he'd draw attention to them in Arshak. If he could shift, Father might take him along. And if leaving his loved ones to join the Cross Scar pride was the price of saving Mother, he'd gladly pay it.

Close to completing a circuit of the city, Zana heard his name being called. Instead of Nahrian, Roshan waved at him. His heart grew heavy, replacing the lightness in his chest. She and Navid stood at the city's well, her brother drawing water. Eager to talk to Nahrian about joining the pride, he didn't have time.

Father didn't think Mother's capture by the high magus was Roshan's fault, even though she'd said otherwise. If he were to make an excuse, make it appear he was avoiding her, she'd think he blamed her for what had happened. He bounded over to the twins and tried his best to smile.

'How's Behrouz?' Roshan asked.

She still feels guilty.

'Father says it isn't your fault. The seal is still powerful, and it's difficult to resist.'

The twins raised their eyebrows. They weren't expecting such an answer.

Roshan bent down and gave him a hug. He thought he might blush. The ache between his temples, however, eased.

'You're worried about him,' she said, and then let go.

The twins sat down with their backs pressed against the well. Zana found himself as eager to talk as he was to find Nahrian.

'I've never seen Father this way,' he said. 'He looks ready to hurt someone and then, suddenly, he looks as if he'll cry. He won't get better until Uncle Emad lets us leave Baka and rescue Mother.'

Navid's eyes narrowed, and he tilted his head.

'You said *us*. So, you're going with Behrouz?'

Zana recognised an opportunity. He'd asked her before, but Roshan had told him to speak to Mother and Father first.

'I can't go like this. I have to shape-shift like you, Navid. The last time I was here, I needed a drink. The woman living in the house over there had to help me lift the bucket out of the well.' He took a deep breath, regarded Roshan with his most anguished expression and said, 'If you could do for me what you did for Navid, I could be of more help to Father.'

She didn't turn away from him. That had to be a good sign.

'What's going on?' Navid said.

Roshan turned.

Zana wanted to bite a chunk out of Navid. Instead, he followed Roshan's stare.

People passed them and headed towards the ziggurat.

Father? Had something happened?

As if she'd heard his thoughts, Roshan said, 'It's Emad. He's called another meeting.'

Brother and sister touched their bracelets and then stood. Both appeared troubled.

If it didn't involve Father, he'd be better off continuing his search for Nahrian. Roshan hadn't answered his question, and from the looks of things, she wouldn't answer it now. He still had a chance. He'd ask her later, when she wasn't distracted. If learning to shape-shift took too long, Roshan's magic was an option.

'Something's wrong,' Roshan said. Her fingertips remained pressed to her bracelet. 'I think Emad's hurt.'

Zana sighed. Finding Nahrian would have to wait.

The three of them joined the throng of djinn as they marched towards the square facing the ziggurat. Parents carried children. The older ones ran to keep up with them. People spoke, but in hushed voices. They, too, must have felt Uncle's pain. Something bad had happened.

'This way,' Navid said. He led them away from the crowd and down a side street on their right.

'Where are you going?' Roshan said.

'I know a shortcut. I'm helping to map the city, remember,' he said, then began to run.

Zana and Roshan raced after him. At the end of the street they turned left, the city's east wall casting them in shadow. The sound of the sea breaking onto the shore came over the wall.

They ran some hundred paces, and then Navid turned left and down a paved, narrow passageway. Ahead of them, above the surrounding buildings, rose the second and third tiers of the ziggurat.

Just before the passageway opened out onto a square facing the ziggurat, Navid skidded to a halt. He waited until they'd caught up, then pointed at a staircase on their left.

'Come on,' he said, and mounted the steps.

The top of the stairs opened onto a balcony with a balustrade. While Zana couldn't see over it, the square and the ziggurat in front of them were visible between the balusters. If they'd stood in the square below, he wouldn't have seen a thing.

Zana nodded his thanks to Navid, who winked.

A hush settled over the square.

With his back to the djinn crammed into the square, Uncle Emad climbed the stairs, a box tucked under one arm. He stopped, turned and stared at a point above the crowd.

Uncle Emad kept blinking, and Zana found his own eyes tearing up. He glanced up and to his side. Roshan resting her head on Navid's shoulder.

Uncle Emad looked up at the sky and closed his eyes, making his face crease. He took two breaths and then opened his eyes. Still, he didn't look at the djinn.

'Citizens of Baka and manticores,' he said, his sonorous voice filling the square, 'your king, my brother, is dead.'

6

Roshan leaned on the balustrade. The death of the king had knocked the wind out of her. Iram and King Fiqitush were gone. The djinn could never go back. Although she'd only known him for a week, she'd wept alongside the djinn who filled the square.

Time slowed, sped up, stopped—Roshan couldn't tell which. Together with Navid, Zana and the djinn, she grieved, and it had left her exhausted.

'Citizens of Baka, manticores.'

Roshan sighed. She found herself cross-legged on the floor of the balcony, nestled between Navid and Zana. Roshan remembered none of them sitting down. Her eyes had dried, and she wiped her cheeks with the back of her hands. Across from her, Emad stood halfway up the ziggurat's steps. In his right hand he held up a box, a box used for holding a clay tablet.

Emad gazed up from the djinn at the northernmost mountain.

'He's not just talking to the djinn,' Zana whispered. 'He knows manticores are on that mountain and they're listening.'

'My brother is dead, but his vision lives on. This tablet

contains that vision, and it is a wonderful vision. Baka is *alive*. For now, it sleeps. But when it awakens, it will rise above the ground and—like any of us—it will pass through a portal. Our king has given us a means to escape the high magus.'

A murmur rippled through the crowd.

Navid's arm enclosed her before she slid from under herself.

'Roshan, are you all right?' he said. 'Your hand.'

She looked down to see Zana sniffing her right hand as it cupped her knee. Her skin was blue-grey, and beneath it, strips of orange whirled.

After what Manah had told her, this had to be Domain power changing her.

The orange whirls turned on both the back and front of her hand. Roshan tugged her tunic's cuff and checked beneath her undershirt. The blue-grey colour and the orange energy covered her forearm. She touched a cheek.

'Is my face...like my hand?' she said to Navid.

'No,' he said. Navid leaned forward and hooked the top of her tunic's neckline with a finger. He pulled it down as far as the dip between her collarbones. 'It stops beneath your neck.' His eyes moved down to her hands. 'What's happening to you?'

Roshan wanted to stuff both hands into her tunic's pockets and hide. The whirls of light radiating from beneath her skin were the same colour as the portal she'd fallen through in Derbicca.

'It's Domain power,' she said. 'It's replenishing my auric energy with sabaoth energy.'

'Is it permanent?' Zana said. 'Will your skin always look this way?'

She hoped not. And was it only her skin the sabaoth energy had altered?

'I never got to ask Manah about the effects. My skin has changed colour before, when I helped Behrouz after the high magus had stabbed him with his golden arrow. The change was temporary.' Roshan held up her hand. 'Now I don't know if or when it will look normal.'

A thought occurred to her and dried Roshan's mouth.

What would happen if Domain power replaced all of my djinn and human auric energy?

The question brought her out in a sweat. If all she could summon was Domain power, she'd have to avoid weaving magic.

While I still have some control, shouldn't I sever the connection between myself and the djinn, go to Arshak and wipe away the high magus and his army?

In her hands, sabaoth magic was like wielding a war hammer to squash an ant. She wouldn't just kill Sassan, she'd obliterate the encampment and everyone in it. Daniyel's death still haunted her. Roshan wasn't sure she could live with the loss of Yesfir and the other captured daevas.

Her skin itched.

Roshan touched her bracelet. She saw Navid do the same. He rose, then helped her up.

'Something's up,' he said. He bent over the balustrade and pointed. 'There—it's Shephatiah.'

Roshan joined her brother. Zana pressed his face between two balusters.

Shephatiah, the djinni whom Roshan thought of as the king's assistant, climbed the ziggurat's steps two at a time. On reaching Emad, he whispered in the prince's ear.

Even from where they stood, Roshan saw Emad's face pale. The two djinn exchanged some words. Shephatiah nodded before disappearing into a portal.

Emad stuck the box under one arm, straightened his tunic and raised his chin.

'Citizens of Baka, manticores,' he said, 'a portal appeared half a league from the city. The high magus has arrived and has begun to pitch camp.'

A wave of panic surged through the square. Roshan's skin itched and the coils of orange beneath it brightened.

'Stay calm,' Emad said, his voice filling the square. 'To panic now would be our undoing. The high magus won't be ready to attack the city until dawn. We have time to prepare Baka and ourselves. We are five hundred *djinn*. Your magic makes each of you a formidable adversary. Together, if we combine our minds and our magic, we will be unconquerable.'

Roshan felt Emad's conviction flow through her bracelet. Her skin didn't prickle so much. Below, the djinn stood rapt. They experienced Emad's emotion and his belief they could resist the high magus, his army and the seal.

'Defences team,' Emad said, 'the high magus can raise portals. I want a dome of protection raised to prevent his soldiers from entering Baka. The rest of you, you have your tasks. Baka must be defendable and habitable by dusk. Now go!'

The djinn turned and departed the square, some on foot and others through portals.

Roshan clutched the balustrade to steady herself. With High Magus Sassan outside the city, the magic required to protect Baka from an assault would take its toll on her.

'Has anyone been assigned this place?' she asked Navid, pointing at the door behind them.

He pulled back a shutter and peered through the window.

'I don't think so.'

Roshan turned. Her legs wobbled.

'Good,' she said. 'I need to go and lie down.'

7

Sassan stepped out of the recently erected operations tent. Across the sand, light from the setting sun glinted off Baka's copper doors.

Those doors weren't there when we arrived, he thought.

He glanced up and to his left at the five golems—one complete and the other four lacking arms or a head. Cast with from the surrounding sand and rock, they resembled a giant version of the statues seen around Persepae. It was late afternoon when he'd seen the finishing touches being added to the first golem. When it reached Baka's walls, the golem's bearded head, based on the emperor's features, would—his magus and Afacan's engineer had assured him—peer over the battlements. By morning, the golems would all be ready to march.

The golems weren't the entire reason for his confidence. Earlier in the day, he'd received a tablet from the emperor confirming his support and willingness to provide as many men as he needed. Sassan considered it another sign from God.

'High Magus.'

General Afacan had exited the operations tent and

approached. From the quickness of his step, Sassan figured the general wanted something.

'Yes, General?'

The general stopped in front of him. He glanced at the tower-like viewing platform being constructed behind Sassan. Above the wheels, the engineers had added a second tier, the wood brought in from a woodyard in Persepae.

The general returned his attention to Sassan.

'High Magus, could I have one last portal raised?' He gestured at the golems and the tower. 'With all the men over here preparing for tomorrow's assault, I'd like to transport some extra men from Arshak for tonight's guard duty.'

Sassan felt as if he were sinking. He had to place his hands behind his back so the general wouldn't see him squeeze his fists around the golden arrow.

'The djinni, Yesfir, is exhausted, General. She needs rest.'

The general nodded.

'What about the daeva, Dunanu? He's helped with the transport of men between Arshak and here.'

With Tamraz missing, Dunanu was his replacement. Unlike the previous daeva, Dunanu fought the seal's influence, which made being a conduit between the seal and the daeva excruciating. Now not only did he experience his insides being liquified, also his bones snapped, re-knit and fractured for as long as the portal held.

Sassan's vigorous head shaking made him dizzy.

The general put out a hand to steady him.

'Are you all right?'

Afraid he'd appear weak, he stepped away from Afacan.

'Thank you, I am, General. Like Dunanu and Yesfir, I need to rest.' He tilted his head at the golems. 'There won't be any more portals until the morning. I'll speak to my magi and make sure one of those fellows keeps watch tonight.'

The general gave a stiff nod.

'I know you're tired, High Magus, but I have a question. I hope you'll answer it before retiring for the evening.'

The general had been huffy with him since he'd first tried the seal out on Pudil and Ninib. It wouldn't do to further antagonise him.

'Let's walk to my tent. On the way, you can ask your question.'

The general agreed. They hadn't gone far when Afacan asked it.

'During the meeting, we discussed the different ways of breaching Baka's walls. I'm pleased you understand that tomorrow's first assault is a test of the city's defences. But if we're able to break into the city and take it, what do we do with the daevas inside Baka?'

Sassan knew the general was looking for confirmation of their conversation in Derbicca. He also knew he was about to contradict himself, but he didn't care.

'I want every daeva manacled.'

The general faltered.

'Do you intend on having them all executed?'

Sassan still thought the general indulged the daevas. Perhaps it was a good thing. Maybe God worked through the general and tempered Sassan's initial response to the djinn rescuing that daeva, Emad.

'Don't worry about the daevas, General. I won't execute them. Yesfir and Dunanu are two examples of how the djinn and daevas will work to make the empire stronger. Once we take Baka, I'll set them to work—God's work and the empire's work.' Sassan's chest puffed. 'In Derbicca, I had every intention of executing them—all of them. But that was before God sent me this.' He raised his hand. The seal's edge glinted in the fading light. 'The seal has changed things. There's work that needs doing, and the daevas will help us do it.'

The general halted.

'What kind of work, High Magus?'

Sassan continued past the general. Now wasn't the time for an explanation and the inevitable barrage of questions.

'I'm tired, General. We shall discuss this after you've taken Baka and the daevas are our prisoners.'

The general soon caught up with him.

'Whatever my men's involvement in this work is, High Magus, I will have to check first with the emperor before assisting you.'

Eager for this conversation to end, Sassan nodded.

'I understand, General,' he said.

They walked the rest of the way in silence. The thought of putting the daevas to work dulled the continuous needle-sharp jabs to his head and neck.

He recalled what he mistook for a dream he'd had last night. It wasn't a dream but a vision the seal had shared with him. He stood in Solomon's place and beheld a great temple erected by the djinn. It reached three storeys, slit-like windows running along its walls. Two bronze pillars fronted the temple's porch. Behind the porch stood double doors inlaid with golden flowers, cherubim and palm trees. Before he'd risen from his bed, Sassan had decided he would build an even grander high temple in Persepae.

Outside his tent, Sassan wished the general good night. Inside, he slumped with relief when he saw a fresh amphora on the table.

He pulled off his tunic and sat down at the table. Sassan poured some water into a drinking bowl. He scratched the sealing wax off with a fingernail, careless of several flakes falling into the bowl, uncorked the amphora and dribbled a little of the opaque liquid into the clear water. Sassan added more, corked it and set the amphora down.

He swirled the contents and sat back.

'I'll build You a temple beyond compare, Divine Light,' he

said. 'Seen from the inside or the outside, everyone will recognise Your glory.'

Sassan stopped himself from raising the bowl in salute. That would be disrespectful. He sat back, took a sip of the bitter mixture, closed his eyes and pictured himself directing the daevas as they raised a glorious new temple.

8

B y the time they reached Baka's west-facing ramparts, the sun had begun to set behind the high magus's encampment. It shone behind the five golems and cast long grey shadows across the sand.

For the past six hours, the djinn had used magic to restore the city's battlements. All five hundred of them now occupied over half of its buildings. To the east, out on the water, two triremes, their sails furled, lay anchored. Emad had overseen their construction. One of them was now home to the djinn's children. Should guardsmen overrun the city, the ships were the djinn's final means of escape.

Except for those on guard, most of the djinn had retired to their new homes. They occupied only the upper floors as a precaution ordered by Emad. Rope-and-plank walkways, strung between all the buildings, converged on the ziggurat, the djinn's fallback. If guardsmen breached the battlements, the ziggurat was where they'd make their last stand before Emad gave the order to retreat to the ships.

Thanks to their magic, they'd achieved so much.

'They won't be easy to stop,' Roshan said.

Navid frowned.

'Who are you talking about?'

Roshan stared at the golems in their different stages of completion.

'The golem inside Iram was a fraction of their size. If I hadn't channelled more energy into Behrouz, it would have been unstoppable. Everyone is pleased with what they've achieved. I'm not sure they understand how dangerous those things are.'

Navid chewed his lower lip.

'They're just tired. Speaking of which, you look exhausted. You should get more rest.'

What she wanted to do was to fight. If she took off her bracelet and disconnected herself from the djinn, she'd wipe away those golems with a thought and then rescue Yesfir and the daevas. If it didn't take all her energy just to stand upright and walk in a straight line, she would have.

'You're right,' she said, hiding her frustration. 'We should go back.'

Roshan turned to go. With her back to Navid, she glanced at her hands. The change had started around noontime and soon after he'd announced the king's death. More orange strands of shimmering light appeared beneath her blue-grey skin around mid-afternoon. As they applied themselves to their tasks, she'd felt their work draw more of her energy.

Domain power will replenish the energy you pass on, leaving your aura filled with sabaoth energy, Manah had said. He'd also said it would leave her tired, but he'd never explained how it would change her.

They reached the stairs leading down to the city's doors, their surfaces covered with thick sheets of copper. Wards pressed into the metal protected the doors from human magic and battering rams. A dozen djinn sat with their backs against the doors, shovels at their feet, waiting for darkness to descend so they could leave the city.

As Roshan and Navid made their way to their room overlooking the ziggurat and square, not everyone had disappeared into their appointed homes. A group worked outside a storeroom suspended above dozens of short pillars. While pairs of djinn conjured grain, others shovelled the cereal into portals, their destination windows directly above three chutes in the storeroom's roof. They stopped work when they saw Roshan, and bowed.

The djinn returned to work, and the strands of orange that covered the back of Roshan's hands whirled and brightened. She slid her hands into her tunic's pockets to avoid anyone noticing.

Closer to the ziggurat, they stopped at one of the inactive wells. Three djinn had climbed down into it, using a ladder with a dozen rungs. She joined Navid, who peered over the well's edge. All three shovelled sand into a portal, its glowing rim illuminating the bottom of the shallow well.

'It looks like there's a granite base,' Navid said. He examined the well's sides. 'There's nowhere for water to permeate.'

Roshan yawned.

Navid led her away by the elbow.

'Come on,' he said. 'Solving the mystery of Baka's wells will have to wait.'

Firestones, hung from under the rope walkways, began to glow the deeper they went into the city. The djinn sat on their roofs, huddled around activated firestones, and spoke in thin murmurs. The sound reminded Roshan of when she was a novice and shared a dormitory. Some novices would continue talking after firestones out, and Roshan would fall asleep to the sound. Her eyelids grew heavy at the memory.

'Navid, Roshan.'

Roshan glanced up. Zana's head gazed down at them.

'We're on our way home,' Navid said. 'Roshan's tired.'

Roshan smiled at Navid calling the room *home*.

Above her, Zana's expression hinted at disappointment and some annoyance.

Her guilt over what had happened to Yesfir jerked her back into wakefulness.

'It's all right,' she said to both of them. 'We can go up—just for a little while.'

She ignored Navid when he shook his head.

'The door's open,' Zana said, and then disappeared.

The second floor of the terraced house was open-plan. Except for the hearth, scattered rugs covered the stone floor. Between the hearth and the bed pressed against the back wall sat a semicircle of divans. Windows in three of the walls let in natural light. Above them, firestones lined an alcove that circled the room and filled it with peach-coloured light.

Roshan's chest ached. This was the home Behrouz wanted to share with Yesfir.

They found him and Zana on the roof. Behrouz sat on a cushion in front of a low table. A jug and some glasses sat on the tabletop.

He's shrunk, Roshan thought.

Behrouz stood and gave them a sad smile. He waved them over.

'Come, sit,' he said. 'I've just woven some pomegranate juice. It's Yesfir's favourite, but Zana can't stand it. I'm still trying to perfect the sweetness.'

Roshan positioned her cushion so she could sit closer to Behrouz. She waited until he'd poured them a drink. Zana declined a refill. The juice was cool and sweet.

'It's good,' Navid said. 'I think the sweetness is just right.'

Behrouz's smile didn't reach his eyes. Roshan saw how his right knee bounced beneath the table.

'How are you?' she said, then placed her hand on his.

He shrugged.

'I can't feel her with this.' He tapped his bracelet. 'But I know she's in that encampment. She's here, but outside the city.'

Roshan touched her bracelet. Sure enough, all she registered was Yesfir's existence, nothing to suggest her physical or mental state.

'She must be under a dome of protection,' Navid said.

Behrouz nodded. His knee-bouncing increased.

'Emad came to see me,' Behrouz said. He stared at his glass. 'He said that, for now, there's nothing we can do for Yesfir. And then he told me what her father had said before he'd died. The king said Yesfir would sacrifice herself if it prevented others from being captured.'

Roshan felt sick. She squeezed Behrouz's hand.

'I'm so sorry,' she said. 'If I hadn't hesitated—'

Behrouz shook his head.

'Don't be. I've spent the last seven years as a daeva while Yesfir remained a djinni. During that time, I never resented her for having the auric energy I lacked. I was strong enough to resist my urges. Otherwise, I could never have remained with her.' He shook his head again. 'But the seal is something else. I couldn't resist the control it had over me. If you hadn't have brought me back to Iram, the high magus would have two djinn to control. I have to bide my time, and you have to keep channelling your auric energy. For now, we have a city to defend.'

Roshan exchanged a glance with her brother. Behrouz believed what he'd said, but the truth of it ate away at him, leaving him anxious.

'Mother must be so tired.'

Roshan hadn't seen Zana skirt the table to sit beside her.

'She must have raised so many portals for so many soldiers to be here,' he continued. His tears glimmered in the firestones' light.

Roshan hugged him. She ignored how one of his quills snagged her tunic.

'Isn't there anything you can do to help her?' Zana said. He began to cry.

She bit her cheek to stop her own tears.

'The djinn need my help to prepare the city,' she said. 'But when the time is right, I will take off my bracelet and I will go into the encampment, and I will use all the magic I know to bring back Yesfir. I promise you, Zana. Until then, we mustn't give up on her. We have to be patient and wait for the right moment.'

She hugged Zana. Like Behrouz, she'd spoken the truth. And like Behrouz, it didn't calm her anxiousness.

9

Armaiti hovered above the rooftop of Behrouz's home. Below, the djinni reached across and examined the blue-grey skin of Roshan's hand and the whirling strands of orange light beneath. His concern for her was plain from his posture. He no longer slumped but sat up, his shoulders straight and his eyes focussed on Roshan.

Armaiti had taken a risk steering Roshan towards channelling her auric energy to the djinn and daevas. If Roshan became more sabaoth than human or djinni, it didn't matter so long as she continued to channel her energy. The Unmade Creator's lack of intervention, however, mattered. It mattered a lot, because fooling Roshan, transforming her aura, and doing it with impunity, suggested this was what the Unmade Creator wanted Armaiti to do. Had free will guided Armaiti's actions, or had It predetermined her reaction to her punishment?

'Does it hurt?' Behrouz said, examining Roshan's hand.

'Apart from a little itching, not really,' Roshan said. 'The colour fades whenever groups of djinn change shifts and no one's weaving magic. It also flared when the djinn congregated in the square earlier this afternoon.' She gazed at Behrouz. 'Even if it doesn't fade, it'll be worth it.' Roshan's head drooped forward. She shook her head. 'According to the sabaoth, Manah, it's the only way I can help the djinn without harming them.'

If she'd adopted a corporeal form, Armaiti's delight would have sent shivers through her body.

'Are you listening to this, Manah?' she said, addressing a domain beyond her own. 'The stupid girl thinks I'm you.'

If the Unmade Creator didn't approve of what she was doing, Manah would appear within seconds. Then she'd have the proof she needed that what she was up to was wrong.

She waited and listened to Roshan describe her time in the basin with the sabaoth she took for Armaiti's enemy. Disguised as Manah, Armaiti had spoken the truth about Domain power and avoiding thoughts that could be open to interpretation. However, she had failed to explain—omitted—that a mind unencumbered by a human or djinn brain required less time to master sabaoth magic. Her omission left Roshan overthinking things and doubting herself.

Time passed, and neither the Unmade Creator nor Manah intervened. Manah's absence and Its continued punishment of Armaiti for saving the infant Roshan pointed at her being played. Everything she'd done and had gotten away with was part of Its complex, unknowable plan.

The realisation left Armaiti sorely tempted to stop interfering and leave Roshan, Sassan and everyone else to do whatever they pleased.

Then you're spiting yourself. Roshan will continue to live a very long time, and you'll remain stuck on this suffocating world until it's dust.

Armaiti began to rise. She'd heard enough. The more Roshan channelled her energy, the weaker she'd become. When she was weak enough, Armaiti would strike. And then, not even the sabaoth energy couched within Roshan's aura would save her. Drained of auric energy, Domain energy would overwhelm her djinn and human body as it tried to save her. Roshan would disappear in a puff of smoke, *permanently.*

10
---

*Z*ana listened as Roshan described what made her skin change colour. Four days earlier, he'd asked Roshan for help with shape-shifting. He understood now why she'd told him to first talk to Mother and Father. Roshan couldn't control the magic she wove.

With Father and Roshan unable to help Mother, he had to do something. If he stood any chance of rescuing Mother, he needed to shape-shift, and the only person he knew who could help him with that was Ramina.

Unsure if Father would allow such a thing, Zana decided it was best not to ask and just go.

He excused himself with a nod to Father. To avoid raising suspicion, he walked casually, as if he were only going downstairs to find something to eat.

Below, in the living area, he gazed at the semicircle of divans. What would it have been like, the three of them living here? Zana shook the thought away and padded down the stairs.

The light spilling out from the buildings he passed and from the firestones overhead, made the streets feel cheery, until Zana remembered the giant golems and the army encampment visible from the battlements. Behind him, a light shone from the second and third tiers of the ziggurat. According to Father, djinn were up there maintaining a protective portal over the city.

Halfway to the west-facing doors, he passed djinn standing over one well. Inside, a djinni hammered and then complained his magic-hardened pick hadn't scratched the bottom. Farther on, and closer to the doors, a group of djinn recited incantations for creating bows and arrows.

By the time he reached them, the copper-lined doors were closed. What had he expected?

The east sea-facing wall and its smaller door weren't so well guarded. The door led to the beach below and also provided access to the northernmost mountain's slope. Zana plotted a route that avoided passing Father's and Mother's house. Satisfied he knew a way, Zana turned.

Father stood in front of him, his hands on his hips.

'Out for a walk?' he said.

Zana's face reddened, and he pursed his lips. Father was kind-hearted, not stupid. He knew Zana was up to something, and deserved the truth.

'I'm going to see Ramina, the leader of the Cross Scar pride. She's offered to teach me how to shape-shift.'

Father's raised eyebrow reminded Zana of Mother.

'So, you thought the night before an empire attack was a good time to end up lost on a mountain?'

Impatience fuelled Father's words. He had to be careful not to turn his impatience into anger.

'Ramina said she'd teach me. If I can shape-shift, then I can enter the encampment during a battle.' He described his plan to disguise himself as an empire soldier and search for Mother.

The creases between Father's eyebrows softened, and his hands slid from his hips. He gestured to his right and at a line of stalls for housing pack animals.

Once inside a stall and out of earshot, Father said,

'That's'—he paused to search for a word—'very brave of you, Zana. Even if you were able to shape-shift, I couldn't just let you wander around the enemy's encampment. I'm worried enough as it is about your mother. I don't want to worry about you, too.'

Tears welled before Zana spoke.

'I know about the ships Uncle Emad built. If the soldiers break into the city, we're all going to sail away on them. Is that true?'

Father nodded.

'Then what about Mother? If someone doesn't rescue her, she'll be the high magus's slave. She'll die a slave, Father. We have to do something.'

Father folded his arms.

'And you don't think I already know that?' He raised his forearm and the bracelet he wore. 'If I didn't have to wear this to bring back Mother, if I could rescue her without the need for djinn magic, I'd go right now. But I'd be fooling myself if I believed I could do it on my own.' He sighed. 'It will take more than one of us.'

Zana felt his chest flutter.

'If I can shape-shift, we can rescue her together. I'd wear your bracelet until you needed it.'

For several heartbeats, Father's eyes brightened. Then he sighed again.

'No,' he said. 'If anything happened to you, I'd never forgive myself.'

Zana wanted to collapse onto his haunches. He was getting nowhere.

'I'm sorry, Father,' Zana said. 'I have to rescue Mother.'

Zana bolted past Father, out of the stall, and raced into a dark alleyway.

He had one chance. Although they'd rebuilt the ramparts, he hoped that the djinn hadn't yet cleared away the sand banked up against the north-facing wall. Zana had seen Nahrian use it that first afternoon he'd followed her.

Zana ignored Father's calls and kept to the shadows. If Father saw him, he would cut him off using a portal or some other magic. He spotted the stairs up to the ramparts on his right. Darkness hid the first five steps. Zana waited at their foot and listened for Father's calls. He'd climb once Father had his back to him. Otherwise, Father only had to look up and he'd be done for.

Even if he catches me, I'll try again tomorrow, he promised himself.

Father's voice echoed off walls, making it hard to fix his location. The desperation and regret Zana detected in his voice tore at him. Mother's capture had crushed him. What would his disappearing into the mountains do to Father? Zana squeezed his eyes shut and listened. Father had passed him.

Zana pelted up the steps, taking them two at a time. Halfway up, his hind foot slipped. If it weren't for his claws, he would have tumbled backwards. His heart pounded inside his head and sounded like it had doubled its rate after his slip. Zana breathed through his open mouth and bounded up and up.

He reached the walkway, half-expecting Father to be waiting for him. Zana found the ramparts ahead of him empty.

'Hey, Zana! What are you doing up here? Didn't you hear Behrouz calling you?'

Zana glanced over his shoulder. A djinni approached, a quiver hanging from his belt and a bow slung over one shoulder.

Zana didn't answer. He raced forward. All he had was the two-day-old memory of his first encounter with Nahrian. If he was wrong about the location, or if the djinn had been thorough and had cleared away the sand on the other side of the wall, he'd either injure himself or plunge to his death.

Zana let instinct guide him.

11

Emad sat on the steps beneath the ziggurat. Most of the djinn had returned to their new homes to eat and to rest. They'd achieved so much in such a short time, but they were exhausted. Regardless of the encampment and the golems, people would sleep. With that in mind, Emad had set hourly watches—any longer and those on duty would fall asleep while standing.

'You'd be proud of what they've achieved, Fiqitush,' he whispered.

Emad closed the box containing his brother's tablet and scanned the square. He bowed his head and then wiped his eyes. Emad hadn't had time to mourn his brother's passing.

'I understand your dream for our people now, brother.' He shook his head. 'I'll never rule them, but—for you—I'll lead the djinn towards making your vision a reality. I just hope your belief in me is well placed.'

He looked up when he heard footsteps. The twins had entered the square. Emad opened the box and made a show of studying the tablet inside. With half an hour to pass before the war council convened, he planned on using the time for some reflection. With Roshan and Navid drawing closer, he wasn't sure if he wanted company.

'Emad,' Navid called.

He feigned surprise and waved.

That's done it, he thought when he saw them approach.

Emad remembered his promise to Fiqitush.

From their lined brows, he could tell this wasn't a social visit.

'We've just seen Behrouz,' Navid said.

Roshan elbowed her brother.

'Emad's busy,' she said. 'Can't you see that?'

Emad smiled.

'I understand, Navid,' he said. 'If I were Behrouz, I'd be unhappy—no, I'd be frustrated by the lack of effort behind Yesfir's rescue. No one's sure where she is. Once the rest of the high magus's army arrives, I'm sure Yesfir will be in one of the prisoner tents. Depending on how things go tomorrow, and if we're able to keep the high magus busy, we'll see about getting her back.' He frowned before Navid could interrupt. 'It isn't a great plan. For now, it's the best I can do. We're stretched and everyone's tired.' He waved a finger at them. 'That includes you two. Shouldn't you be inside, a meal in your bellies and resting?'

Navid nodded. He pointed up at a balcony.

'We were just on our way home.'

'Why don't you join us?'

Emad heard the hesitation and a hint of sorrow in Roshan's voice. He didn't need his bracelet to tell she felt sorry for him, sitting out here on his own, his brother not yet gone a full day.

'Thank you, Roshan,' he said, wishing he could hug her. 'I have a war council meeting soon.' He tapped the box resting on his lap. 'I was searching for a way to revive Baka, to get it to rise high enough to pass through a portal. Fiqitush believed it was possible. He told me I'd find proof he hadn't gone mad if I dug away the sand beneath one of its walls.'

Navid took a step forward, his attention fixed on the box.

'Let me guess; Baka's foundations consist of granite, a rock that isn't from around here.'

Emad squinted.

'What have you been digging around for?'

Navid jabbed the space above his shoulder with a thumb.

'I wasn't digging, but I heard a djinni trying to unplug a dry well complain about hitting granite.'

The lad was sharp.

'Which suggests...'

Navid shrugged.

'That the material used to lay Baka's foundations isn't from these parts. Someone dragging granite from one place to another for a city's foundations sounds crazy. A city that can fly, that's crazier.'

Roshan shoved her brother.

'Don't be rude,' she said. 'If King Fiqitush thought Baka could...fly, then it must be true.'

Emad tilted his head at Navid. Roshan was trying too hard to please him.

'I'm inclined to agree with your brother.' He patted the box. 'There is so much information in this tablet, it could take months before I've read it all.'

'So, there's no chance of the high magus stepping out of his tent tomorrow morning to find Baka gone?' Navid said.

I'd give anything to see the look on his face, Emad thought.

'I'm afraid not. As I said, the tablet contains a lot of information: my brother's research and his plans for the future. Because I'm not sure what I'm looking for, it's taking time to get through it all.'

Roshan peered at the box.

'Yesfir taught me a system of symbols she used to organise her entries. She often used an incantation to organise the entries by symbol. Maybe the king had taught her the system.'

Emad winced at the thought of poor Yesfir. He gestured at the step he sat on.

'If you're not too hungry or tired, sit down and have a look.'

He whispered an incantation over the box to allow Roshan access to the entries. Roshan sat on his right with Navid next to her. He handed her the box, then watched her open it. Emad was about to tell them about the entries Fiqitush had made about them, but then he saw Roshan's hand. He reached out and took it in both of his.

'What's happening to you?' he said.

He felt a slight tug as she tried to pull her hand away. He softened his grip. She held the box in both hands and gave him a pained smile.

'It's nothing to worry about.'

He glanced at Navid, who shrugged.

She's too young, too trusting, to be caught up in all this.

Roshan's willingness to help the djinn had side effects. The idea wrenched his insides.

'Unless you're smearing ash on your skin and you want to become an Indus ascetic, I'm right to be concerned—don't you think?'

She probably didn't know what an Indus ascetic was.

Roshan nodded, her lips a thin line. He listened as she described the reason for her skin's colour and the swirling orange light beneath it.

'What do you think about what's happening to your sister?' he said to Navid.

Navid chewed his lip.

'To be honest,' he said, eventually, 'I wish she'd take off her bracelet and rest. But I won't make her. Whatever she wants to do, I'll support her. If she knew a way of making whatever's happening to her stop and she wanted my help, she'd only have to ask.'

Good answer.

So long as Navid watched over her, his caution and concern were unnecessary, suffocating perhaps.

'Navid's right,' Emad said. 'You must rest. Before you go to sleep, take off your bracelet. I'll let everyone know so no one will panic if their powers flag.'

Like her brother, Roshan chewed her lip.

'What about the protective dome around the city?'

He raised a placating hand.

'Don't you fret about that. We've enough djinn and enough auric energy to maintain the dome while you sleep.'

Roshan's gaze shifted between the open box and Emad.

'All right, tonight, before bed, I'll take it off,' she said, then regarded the box.

To spare her any surprise, he said, 'You'll find plenty of entries in there about you two. From what I've read so far, my brother watched over you both.' Emad remembered his promise. He couldn't blandly tell them he was their father. Emad needed a more subtle approach. 'Fiqitush watched over you both, even before you were born,' he added, hoping one of them took the bait.

In the past four days, he'd lost his cousin and his brother. He would have prayed if he thought God cared. Emad's throat constricted. He couldn't bear losing the twins, too.

Navid was the first to bite.

'Are you saying the king knew our parents?'

Emad pointed at the tablet.

'Not everything's in there.' He tapped his temple. 'Everything that happened prior to your births is in here.' He took a deep breath. Brother and sister stared at him. As if his words had turned them to stone, neither moved. 'Your mother's name was Shafira. She was smart, beautiful and an adept magus. Nineteen years ago, when the flames around my eyes were orange and I still captained *Apkallu*, she found me in a tavern and asked for my help.'

The twins remained still while he described how he'd first met their mother and the adventure that followed.

***

'YESFIR VISITED SHAFIRA DURING HER PREGNANCY,' Emad said, drawing his encounter with Shafira to a close. 'Your mother told her how she'd planned for you both to live human lives and how she'd already enrolled you as novices at Persepae's high temple.' Emad steeled himself for what came next. 'No one foresaw the complications, however, and even if Yesfir had been present during your births, your mother lost too much blood too quickly. So, Fiqitush kept his eye on you but also kept his distance. He only sent Yesfir and Behrouz to kidnap you when your ability to hold Core power for long pain-free periods, Roshan, risked drawing attention to you. If the magi discovered your true nature, who knows what the temple would have done with you both.'

He stopped, realising he'd spoken at some length. It was their turn to talk.

The same silence with which they'd listened continued. He'd been too busy talking, remembering, to notice how Roshan had leaned against her brother, her head on his shoulder and her hand in his.

'Yesfir,' Roshan whispered, 'she's our aunt.'

Navid stared up at Emad.

'How long have you known?'

He'd been dreading this question. Whichever way he answered it, he'd present himself as being unworthy of calling himself their father. He cleared his throat.

'Two days. It's taken me this long to summon the courage and to find the right time to tell you.'

Roshan sat up. She studied him as if she'd set eyes on him for the first time. Emad tried not to recoil from her scrutiny.

54

'Why didn't you offer to take Shafira with you when you left Tarsa?' she said.

He remembered their last meeting on the dock.

'For the same reason your mother asked Yesfir not to tell me she was pregnant. I wanted to be a ship's captain, and Shafira wanted to be a mother and a magus.' He leaned in and felt his brow pinch. 'Anyway, if I'd asked her to come with me, she would have declined.' He smiled. 'We knew each other for less than a week, but that was long enough to respect what the other valued.' He felt his throat tighten and had to clear it again. 'Shafira, your mother, was an intelligent, talented and courageous woman,' he continued. 'I'm so sorry you never got the chance to know her, and I apologise for my selfishness preventing Shafira and my brother from telling me about you both.'

There, brother, I kept my promise.

Emad reached across and closed the box.

'You're both tired and, if you don't mind me saying so, you look shocked.' He patted the box. 'I'll hold on to the tablet for now. Just ask whenever you want to search through it. What happens next is up to you. Just as I did with your mother, I'll respect your wishes.' He stood when he spotted the first member of the war council enter the square. 'Get some sleep,' he said. 'I'll see you in the morning.'

12

It was too dark for Zana to see anything beyond the parapet he'd hurled himself off. He stretched out his paws. There hadn't been enough time and sufficient light to know if he'd chosen the right spot. All he could do was hope his pads touched sand sooner than later.

His left shoulder struck something solid. He rolled along a slight decline for two heartbeats and then was in mid-air again, the sky overhead. The instant his shoulder scraped against the surface a second time, he extended his claws and dug them into the rock, spraying grit into his face. He moved his legs as if he were trying to climb back up the battlements. Gravity drew him from the wall. Zana dug his claws deeper. His rate of descent slowed, and the gradient turned gentle enough for him to turn without all his limbs losing contact with the surface. Unsure of how far he'd go before hitting the sandy bottom, he stiffened his muscles to slow himself further.

Zana's front paws touched sand. Instinct made him tuck his head in and roll forward to avoid snapping his neck. He landed on his back and then flopped onto his side.

'Zana,' came a call from the walkway above.

With no time to catch his breath, he pushed himself up and onto four legs. Zana turned a full circle to orientate himself. The darkness below made it impossible to know whether he faced north or south. Above him, the city's lights brushed the tips of the crenellated battlements. With the city to his right, Zana sidled to his left and tested the ground beneath his feet. He looked up again, this time at the mountain. Nahrian's mother, Ramina, had said he'd find the pride on the northernmost mountain. From what he could see, which wasn't much, thanks to the shadow cast by Baka's wall, the slope he planned on climbing was more of a vertical cliff.

Zana faced the mountain and, using his front paws, crabbed his way along the edge while trying to detect an incline in the vertical rock face.

His joints ached and one shoulder felt raw when he heard the purl of water lapping the pebbled shore.

The sea!

He must have missed a place to start his ascent and had gone too far. If he went any farther, Zana risked stepping over the table of rock Baka was perched on and falling onto the boulders below.

Zana growled. What a mess. Now he'd have to wait until dawn and risk being spotted while he searched for a way up the mountain.

'Zana.'

He halted and pressed himself against the rock. The call came from his right rather than from above.

A soft ball of red light bobbed towards him.

'Zana, it's me, Nahrian.'

On hearing her name, the muscles in his neck and limbs relaxed. His legs wobbled, and he fought the urge to collapse onto his belly. Zana trotted towards the faint glow.

Nahrian wore a firestone, on its lowest setting, like a pendant. They almost bumped noses when he reached her.

'What are you doing here?' he said.

With her face illuminated from below, her smile appeared more ghoulish than mischievous. The corners of her lips fell, and her brow furrowed.

'I heard what happened to your mother,' she said. 'Vul told me you'd be coming to us for help.'

The memory of their climb up the southern mountain and Vul recalling the death of Zana's mother made him shiver.

How much did Vul know about him, and how much of it had he told Nahrian? Zana told himself it didn't matter. Nahrian was there. A lightness filled his chest. He could get the help he needed and rescue Mother.

'Mother's off hunting,' Nahrian said. 'She won't be back until morning.'

Zana had to sit down.

'Does that mean I have to come back tomorrow?'

Nahrian frowned.

'Of course not. You're staying with us until Mother returns.' She turned. 'Come on.'

The sound of waves grew louder. They reached the end of the city's wall, and Zana stopped to take in the sight.

A crescent moon hung above two dart-shaped triremes, their sails furled. What little moonlight there was lit the foam-flecked waves as they broke over the pebbled beach.

'How far does it go, the sea?'

Nahrian stood beside him.

'I don't know, but I never get bored with watching it. Mother said that if those ships sailed straight ahead and kept on sailing, they'd reach land.'

Zana wondered what lay beyond it.

'Hurry up,' Nahrian said. 'It's dinner time.'

If not for Nahrian, he would never had found the short, narrow cave entrance.

'It sometimes floods during high tide,' Nahrian said, leading him down a tunnel, 'but only as far as the first bend.'

The passage made a sharp right and then straightened. Firestones hung from the ceiling, filling the tunnel with a golden light Zana could have mistaken for daylight.

The deeper they travelled, the more apprehensive Zana grew. He didn't know what to expect when he encountered the pride. It took all of his courage to ask Nahrian how he should behave.

'Stick close to me,' she said. 'You've entered Cross Scar territory. If they think you're a threat, the pride won't hesitate— they'll attack you.'

Zana slid across fine sand.

'What should I do, then? I don't want anyone to think that.'

Nahrian faced him, her expression earnest.

'Walk behind me and keep your head bowed. And every five steps—remember, *five* steps—you say, "I am the mistress's servant. I will not harm you."'

'I am the mistress's servant. I will...' His voice trailed off when he caught Nahrian grinning. 'What are you smiling about? Did I say it wrong?'

Nahrian's laugh filled the tunnel. Confused, he stared at her, which made her laugh harder.

'Your face,' she said. 'It's so sweet.' She stopped laughing and bunched her brows. Nahrian pulled back her chin and in a deep voice said, 'I am the mistress's servant.'

He still didn't understand. She laughed again. He'd spent most of last night and all of today worrying about Mother. The days since Roshan had returned injured from Persepae's chancery hadn't been fun either. Not once did he remember laughing. Even though he was the brunt of the joke, her laugh was infectious.

'Me calling you mistress is what's funny—isn't it?'

By the time they'd stopped laughing, he could ignore his aches and his stinging shoulder.

'Just be yourself, Zana,' Nahrian said. 'The males a little older than us will try to intimidate you, and the older ones will ignore you to let you know they aren't threatened by you. That's just the way you males act. You're bigger and stronger and you like to show off about it.'

He wanted to protest and tell her he'd never show off—Mother never tolerated it. Zana remained silent. There was no telling if Nahrian still made fun of him.

Compared to its tiny entrance, the cavern it opened on to stunned Zana.

The cavern's shape reminded him of an egg, with three concentric and tapering tiers rising to the ceiling. A balcony ringed each one. Beyond the balconies Zana saw circular entrances. Chequered blankets covered each entrance, their colour combinations different for each entrance. Some, their blankets drawn back, revealed a space lit from above by firestones. On the lower tier, where Zana stood, he spied a space with a clothes chest, a bedroll, a low table and its floor covered by a rug.

'That's where you'll be staying,' Nahrian said. 'Mother and I are on the third tier.'

They entered the atrium, its polished floor reflecting the light from what looked more like fireboulders than firestones set in the ceiling.

'They're huge,' he said. 'Who recharges them for you?'

Nahrian smirked.

'It's not only magi and djinn who know magic,' she said. 'The pride's lionesses built this den with magic.'

Nahrian pointed at the floor's three circles, their overlapping curves forming a triangle at their centre. The edges of each circle contained symbols Zana hadn't seen on the tablets and papyri the humans and the djinn used.

Nahrian nodded at the two circles closest to them.

'The one on the left is where we sit and eat our meals. The right circle is the school, where students who can shape-shift learn other skills like reading, writing and weaving magic. And the circle in front of us is the nursery. It's where the cubs come to play during the mornings and where the older ones learn how to shape-shift in the afternoons.'

The thought of learning to shape-shift while other manticores watched didn't thrill Zana. He followed Nahrian as she led him to the circle where they'd eat.

'What about the centre?' he said. He pointed at the curved triangle with his chin. 'Is that used for anything?'

'It's where our leaders, the Matrons, meet during council.' Nahrian stopped and indicated he should sit. 'Stay here while I get us some dinner.'

Before he could ask if he could accompany her, Nahrian turned and headed towards a wide opening in the cavern wall. Behind it, two pairs of male and female humans stood in front of a table, ladling food from tall saucepans into bowls and onto plates. The opening was a kitchen.

A bell rang from somewhere.

Women drew back the blanket-like doors. Behind them followed cubs of all ages. The male manticores were exactly that, manticores. Unlike the females, they hadn't shape-shifted. Just as Nahrian had predicted, the older males ignored him as they exited a circular opening at the far end of the cavern. Zana spotted stairs. The adult males sat on the opposite side of the circle. Although he faced them, he couldn't take his eyes off how big they were. The largest male had to be two heads taller than Father. He was muscular, and the sheen from his fur suggested he spent a lot of time grooming himself. His skin was the colour of pale honey. He counted ten males. While they were all of an intimidating size, their skin colour, manes and fur varied in shade. One even had white fur.

Zana hadn't spotted a male's approach. He had ebony skin and a thick, wiry mane of a similar shade.

Vul stood beside Zana. His stern visage make Zana want to edge away from him.

'So, you came.'

Zana swallowed.

'Hello,' he managed.

Vul stared down at him.

'A vow is a solemn and sacred thing,' he said. 'Never make one if there's the remotest possibility of breaking it.'

Zana did his best to hold the manticore's gaze. He looked away only because he wasn't sure how to reply. Zana felt something hard bump against his side. He relaxed when, over his shoulder, he saw Nahrian. A tray filled with bowls hung inside a net, its ends hanging from her mouth.

Vul strolled towards the stairs the other males had used to come down for dinner.

'From the look on your face, I'm guessing that didn't go well,' Nahrian said.

'It could have been better, I suppose.'

Nahrian pushed a bowl in front of him.

'Don't worry. You're not the only one who feels that way about my brother.'

'It's hard to believe you two are related,' Zana said. 'You're both so...different.'

Nahrian's eyes followed Vul as he ascended the stairs.

'If she chooses to, a manticore female can have more than one mate. For one of her mates, my mother chose the pride's seer. Vul got his looks and his gift for seeing the past and future from his father.'

Zana wanted to ask her how she felt about her mother having more than one husband—if that's how the manticores thought of their mates. He hadn't known her long enough to ask such a question.

'Is that why he's so serious?' he asked instead. 'I don't think he likes me.'

Nahrian sniffed the bowl's contents. She settled on her

haunches before she regarded him with what Zana thought was sadness.

'Vul says Mother must allow you to join the Cross Scar pride.' She swallowed. 'He also said that after you've become one of us and wear the pride's mark, you'll break my heart.'

13

Two hours after dawn, three of the five golems began their march on Baka. Sassan leaned forward, rested his free hand on the railing and caused the tower to rock. General Afacan and two of his senior officers next to him appeared unaffected by the viewing platform's wobbles. Sassan's knuckles remained white until the tower came to a standstill. Below him stood three trios of magi, each arranged around a column of rock onto which they'd carved a symbol. The symbol's green glow pulsed in time with their incantations, instructions transmitted to a similar symbol inside the golem they controlled.

Archers marched behind the golems, some of them with red triangular flags strung to their backs. Sassan still thought it a mistake not to have infantry following behind.

Since their arrival yesterday, the djinn had been busy. Sassan had woken early to see the sun rise behind Baka. He thought the djinn might have worked through the night, but the place looked no different to how it had at dusk. A varicoloured dome of protection, its crown above the ziggurat, now covered the city. Its appearance this morning hadn't troubled the general. Before climbing the tower, Afacan had confirmed he'd made no changes to the plan they had discussed yesterday evening.

If the dome didn't concern the general, Sassan didn't see why he should be concerned, either.

Sassan braced himself and pushed off the railing. He avoided jerky movements and gripped the sabaoth's arrow behind his back.

'Now,' the general called down to the line of magi steering the golems.

The middle golem maintained its pace while the two either side of it accelerated.

Sassan's heartbeat kept pace with the two golems, their feet raising clouds of dust. The golem on the left peeled away from its partner.

That wasn't what they'd agreed last night. One of Afacan's officers muttered something. Whatever it was, he sounded unimpressed.

Below, the magi controlling the left golem slowed their incantation. Sassan stiffened and tried to hide his anger and embarrassment.

Just as the golems synchronised their pace, a blue-violet light surrounded the one on the right, causing it to lurch forward and fall. The magi's incantation, their instructions, changed, causing the third and slower golem to come to a stop. The instruction came too late for the second golem. It halted but then toppled forwards as if a felled tree.

'Portals,' the general said.

The first golem had dug its fingers into the sand to stop itself from falling farther into the portal. Thanks to the coordinated effort of the magi operating it, the golem began to climb its way out—until the second golem collapsed on top of it. Both golems disappeared beneath the sand.

Sassan felt his face burn. He glanced over at the general, who cast an impassive gaze at the scene below.

The archers behind the third golem formed a row, knelt and waited with arrows nocked. An officer gave the order and a line of arrows filled the sky. All of them struck and then bounced off the protective dome, some rolling down its sides.

Even though he and everyone else had expected that to happen, Sassan squeezed the sabaoth's arrow.

The archers nocked a second arrow and took aim.

Sassan held his breath.

A second barrage flew into the air.

He forced himself to keep his eyes open.

The iron-tipped arrows penetrated the dome, a quarter disappearing behind Baka's walls.

Sassan breathed out.

The archers rose.

Sassan glanced at the general. Afacan stood with his hands held behind his back.

What's he waiting for? The archers should advance. They're not yet close enough to the city.

The archers slung their bows over their shoulders.

'General, what's—'

The sand in front of the archers erupted and formed a dust cloud. A captain yelled an order, and the archers began to sprint. The golem turned to follow them back.

Mastiffs, composed of sand and twice the size of a guardsman, emerged from the cloud and charged the fleeing guardsmen. The golem stooped and brushed away both a war hound and a handful of archers.

Sassan grabbed the railing and, ignoring how the tower swayed, yelled at the magi below to return the golem to the encampment and nothing more.

The golem straightened. It ignored the war hounds biting and swiping at its ankles.

The thump of feet from below drew Sassan's attention away from the retreat's shouts and screams.

A column of guardsmen marched in pairs and then fanned out to form a protective cordon around the encampment. They locked iron shields and braced themselves.

Sassan looked up and beyond the cordon.

The war hounds maintained their charge, trampling and mauling anyone in their path. One hundred paces from the cordon, two of the dogs burst as if they'd hit an invisible barrier. The other hounds continued regardless. They, too, turned to puffs of dust.

An order was yelled. Those archers who'd made it past the lead war hounds and carried a flag stopped running. They turned and planted a flag where the creatures had fallen.

'Unless it's a portal,' the general said, 'that's how far they're able to control their magic.' As if he'd seen enough, he gestured at the ladder. 'After you, High Magus.'

Inside the operations tent and while the general's direct reports debriefed him, Sassan seethed. It was as if the general knew what the djinn would do, what they'd throw at them. His magi had made him look a fool. He'd had the golems designed to inspire the guardsmen and create fear in those hiding inside Baka. Instead, he was a laughingstock among the guardsmen and Baka.

'All right,' the general said, after the delivery of the final debrief. 'We've tested Baka's external defences. Here's how I want us to prepare for this afternoon's assault.'

Sassan listened to the general's list of instructions. His magi, along with the guardsmen, would be busy for the rest of the morning. He almost offered to recite the eagle-headed spirit's daeva-slaying incantation over the guardsmen's arrows. But then he reminded himself of how he needed as many of them alive as possible to do God's work in Persepae.

He exited the operations tent in a better humour than the one he'd arrived in. The general had kept his opinion of his magi's performance to himself.

You're being too hard on them, Sassan thought. *After all, this morning was about testing the city. The next attack will be different.*

Inside his tent, he pulled off his tunic. The pain's intensity had risen. He picked up the amphora on his table and uncorked it. Half the contents had been drunk last night. He needed to slow down.

Sassan slouched into his chair and swallowed the amphora's contents. He sighed and closed his eyes.

He is inside Baka, a quiver hanging from his hip and a bow in his hand. Djinn rush at him, but he doesn't lift the bow or nock an arrow. He summons the power of the seal and waves them aside. There's just one djinni he's interested in, that he's come for.

He follows the cries of pain, the smell of ash and burning flesh, and strides past the retreating guardsmen.

Standing against the lone wall of a ruined building, a young woman screams. The surrounding guardsmen erupt into pillars of flame. Her face, hands and forearms are the colour of ash. He halts when he sees swirls of orange flame flicker beneath her skin.

The flaming guardsmen collapse into heaps of ash. He retrieves a golden arrow from his quiver, but she's screaming again, the whirls of orange blazing under her skin. The heat coursing through him shrivels his insides. It's difficult to tell if he or the ground beneath him is shaking. His hand trembles as he attempts to nock the arrow. With his arrow secured to the bowstring, he takes aim. A second scream blackens his skin and makes the fat beneath it bubble. He squints to protect his eyes and knows he's too late when his vision turns bright orange. There's only time enough to take one last breath as his muscles and their ligaments roast.

Time enough to release the arrow.

The screaming stops. He can't be sure if it's his own scream or the djinni's that's ended.

There's silence. A cool breeze brushes his cheek. He's still holding the bow, and he feels rubble beneath his sandals.

His eyes open. Burning blue-grey ash spirals upwards and disappears.

'God's work is done,' he says, lowers his bow and turns.

Before him stand the djinn: men, women and children. As one, they bow deeply.

Sassan woke.

Unsure of how long he'd slept, he rubbed his face.

'There's work to be done,' he muttered to himself, and then pulled on his tunic.

Outside his tent, he gazed up at the sky and gauged the sun's position. He'd been asleep for less than an hour. Before he made his way over to his magi, he turned to the pair of guardsmen on guard duty.

'I need a bow and a quiver of arrows,' he said.

14

Roshan ran a finger down the sleeping djinni's shoulder. The incantation knitted the deep muscle first before it sealed the skin to leave a red scar behind. She rose from the bed and looked across the hall in Baka's municipal building—now a makeshift hospital. Roshan took in the dozen djinn who lay injured by iron arrowheads. There'd been no deaths, but the arrows and the sight of the advancing golems had done far more damage to morale than twelve wounded djinn. She'd felt the fear of those weaving magic on the ramparts.

'You look tired. You shouldn't be here.'

Too busy reliving the chill those djinn had experienced, the will and courage required to stay put and not take cover after the second rain of arrows, she hadn't noticed her brother's approach.

She walked towards him. She felt tired.

'I couldn't lie in a bed while the city was being attacked. I decided to come here and use the healing incantations Yesfir taught me.'

Navid waited while she told the head healer she was leaving.

The municipal building sat behind the ziggurat, so the walk back to their room was a short one.

'Have you thought about what Emad told us?' Navid said.

After their first and disastrous meeting in Derbicca, Roshan had considered the change in the prince's behaviour towards her as strange.

'He didn't know about us that first time we met. It explains why, suddenly, he was so protective towards us.'

They climbed the steps up to the balcony. She cast a sideways glance at the ziggurat. Emad and the war council were up there discussing the next steps for Baka's defence.

Inside the room, Roshan lay down and Navid started a fire in the hearth to boil some water.

'It still hasn't sunk in,' Navid said. 'I mean, the prince being our father is the reason why the king watched over us. But I don't understand why Emad would suddenly care when he admitted he was too selfish to have raised us. If you ask me, he's as shocked and as uncomfortable about the whole thing as we are.'

Navid was right. All three of them still struggled with the news.

'What's difficult is knowing the king was our uncle and Yesfir's our cousin,' she said. 'We've gained a family, and now we're losing them.'

Navid stopped tearing off mint leaves from their stalks.

'I never thought of it that way. Do you think Yesfir found it hard not telling us?'

'I don't know,' she said, with a sigh. 'I hope we get the chance to ask her.'

Their talking about Yesfir had reminded Roshan of her frustration with wanting to fight the high magus and channel energy to the djinn. Her constant tiredness annoyed her. What she really wanted to do was fight, strike a swift, hard blow that would kill the high magus and end this madness.

Roshan remained lost in her thoughts, until she heard a knock on the door.

'Can I come in?' came a voice.

It belonged to Behrouz.

Navid opened the door and ushered him in.

'You're just in time,' he said. 'I'm making tea.'

Since seeing him last night, the djinni stood straighter, and he'd lost his haunted, distant look. Working with Emad to defend the city had brought him out of himself, but sadness remained evident in his eyes.

Roshan sat up.

'Any news of Zana?'

Behrouz shook his head. He sat at the table close to the window overlooking the square.

'Somehow, he managed not to break his neck jumping over the battlements. I went down at first light and found two pairs of manticore footprints leading to the beach. They disappeared among the shingle. It looks like Zana's with the manticores.'

Roshan kneaded one sweaty hand and then the other. Yesfir's capture was her fault. Zana jumping off a wall, putting himself in danger to save Yesfir, was also down to her.

Navid carried over glasses stuffed with mint leaves and filled with hot water. He set them on the table.

'Will they teach Zana how to shape-shift?' he said.

Concern flickered across Behrouz's face.

'Whatever they do, I'm hoping they keep him in the mountains and don't allow him anywhere near the encampment.' He shook his head before squinting at Roshan. 'That's not why I'm here. I came to see if you were all right. I'm under orders from Emad to tell you to take off your bracelet for the next hour and rest.'

Roshan glanced at Navid. Now wasn't the best time to ask Behrouz if he knew he was their uncle. She got up and joined them.

'This first attack just tested our defences,' Behrouz continued. 'The next one will be harder, and you'll need all your strength if you want to help us.'

Navid blew on his tea, and then said, 'Can Baka will survive another attack?'

Behrouz rubbed the back of his neck.

'I don't know. It's been centuries since the djinn tribes fought one another. Thanks to the king and his father before him, the djinn have had little reason to fight. Even I don't have enough experience to know what the high magus's soldiers will do.' He pursed his lips. 'If things get bad, we'll take the ships and leave Baka. Emad will take us somewhere far enough away from the empire and the high magus to start a new life. We must hope that Sassan won't be able to figure out how to use the seal against five hundred djinn all at once.'

Navid nodded and waved a hand at the ceiling.

'This city might be special, and it might even fly one day, but there's no point trying to defend it if the djinn get themselves killed.'

Roshan sat back in her chair and listened to Navid and Behrouz discuss the pros and cons of leaving and whether they'd spend the rest of their days as nomads or outcasts, always fearful that Sassan would finally master the seal.

The image of Yesfir standing beside a tent in the Arshak encampment, her arms raised, had seared itself on Roshan's memory. Yesfir had used an incantation that risked harming not only the guardsmen but the daevas. She hadn't hesitated, her resolve evident. It didn't matter who got in her way. All she wanted was to save her husband, Roshan and Navid.

Roshan straightened. Although she could sleep for a week, her decision eased her stiff muscles. Roshan removed her bracelet to replenish her auric energy.

If Baka's situation grew dire—and the djinn could no longer defend themselves—she'd stop channelling auric energy and go after the high magus. Like Yesfir, she understood that others might also get hurt. When it came time to strike that blow, she wouldn't hesitate.

15

U p on the northernmost mountain, Zana and Nahrian perched on a wide ledge overlooking both the encampment and the city. High enough to be hidden but close enough to recognise those below in Baka, Zana had kept an eye out for Father. Earlier that morning, he'd watched Father tracing his footprints in the sand between the city and mountain's edge. Father had made it only as far as the beach. He'd then stepped through a portal and ended up outside the ziggurat. A little while back, and after the fighting, Zana had seen Father re-emerge to make his way over to where Roshan and Navid lived.

He and Nahrian had watched the attack. The golems disappearing into the portal had filled him with hope. The second volley of arrows penetrating the dome had snatched that hope away.

Last night, after they'd eaten—the goat meat rarer and less flavoursome and spicy compared to Mother's cooking—Nahrian had led him to the room Ramina had allocated him. Together, they'd sat on a rug with a chequered pattern that complemented the blanket covering the room's entrance. There were a table and a chair and a bed, all designed for a human. Zana had enjoyed her company, but he would have enjoyed it more if he'd been able to forget what Vul had said about his mother and what he'd do to Nahrian: he'd broken his mother's heart and he was likely to do the same to Nahrian's. For the rest of the evening, he'd avoided the subject, having got the impression she'd regretting mentioning it. When the time came for her to leave, Zana's insides turned hollow. He missed Mother, and he felt awful for leaving Father the way he did.

'There must be a thousand tents in that camp,' Nahrian said, returning Zana to the present. 'It'll take you forever to search them all.'

Zana had shared his idea with her last night. If he were to steal a guardsman's uniform and search the encampment, he had to know how to shape-shift. The idea seemed so straightforward until, sitting on the mountainside, he saw the encampment's size.

'It might be easier if there was someone else with you,' Nahrian said.

His eyes widened.

'Who were you thinking of?' he said, not wanting to assume anything.

Two notches marked Nahrian's brow.

'Me, stupid.'

Zana shook his head. He understood why Father refused to let him rescue Mother. Just like Father worried about him, Zana wouldn't let anything bad happen to Nahrian.

'Not a good idea.'

Nahrian bumped a shoulder against him.

'Why not?'

'Because human soldiers are all male and you're a girl.'

His observation didn't discourage Nahrian.

'I'll wear a helmet to cover my hair,' she said. 'No one will know.'

Zana wanted to say they would. Her smooth skin and large eyes would give her away.

'No one will know what?'

Zana recognised the voice. He stood and then turned.

Ramina and two other women stood on the path leading to the ledge. Behind them, a female manticore waited. Four goats, their hind legs lashed together to form pairs, hung from the manticore's back.

Nahrian padded over to Ramina, her tail curling and uncurling.

'Zana wants to learn how to shape-shift and save his mother, and I'm going to disguise myself as a soldier and help him.'

Zana's face burned, and he wished Nahrian would shut up. This wasn't how he'd planned on making his request for help. Concerned the pride's leader might not understand what was going on, he stepped forward.

'The high magus has my mother,' he said. 'I want to rescue her, but the only way I can do that is to shape-shift. If you agreed to help me, and once Mother is safe, I will remain with the Cross Scar pride.' He cast a sideways glance at Nahrian. 'While I would be grateful for your help with shape-shifting, I won't risk members of the pride to rescue Mother.'

Ramina crossed her arms and raised her chin.

'Then you're a fool, Zana.' She shook her head. 'If it means sending you to certain death, I'm not prepared to teach you.'

Zana's jaws tightened and his throat constricted. With no one prepared to help him, was this how Father felt?

Zana bowed—he wouldn't embarrass himself further.

'Thank you for your concern. If that's how you feel, I should leave.'

Ramina's eyes bored into Zana.

'And after you've left, what will you do?'

Now she'd refused him, he wanted to tell her it was none of her business. Nahrian had been kind to him and had befriended him. He wouldn't say anything to embarrass her or make himself appear ungrateful.

'When the fighting starts, I'll look for Mother.'

'That's stupid,' Nahrian said. 'You'll never find her on your own. You'll get yourself killed.'

Ramina gestured at the two women behind her. They took a step towards Zana.

'If you try to leave, I'll have you restrained.' She held up a placatory hand. 'I'll make you an offer, Zana, but I can't do that with you walking away from me. Will you listen?'

A lightness filled Zana's chest. He nodded his agreement.

The corners of Ramina's eyes creased.

'If you join the pride, then it is the Cross Scar's responsibility to protect *your* pride, Zana. Nahrian is right; such an undertaking on your own is madness. Four of the pride's lionesses and lions will accompany you into the enemy's camp.' She turned to face her daughter. 'Since you're so eager to help, Nahrian, and you're ready for your first kill, you will also accompany him.'

Nahrian's smile was infectious. Zana couldn't believe what he'd heard. He reminded himself that their help didn't guarantee finding Mother, but with six of them searching for her, the chances of rescuing Mother had increased significantly.

'Thank you,' he said to Ramina first and then Nahrian.

Although he didn't want to put Nahrian at risk, he was glad she was coming with him. When this was over, he hoped she'd help him settle into his new life with the pride.

Ramina rested her hands on her hips.

'Then it's agreed. Both of you wait here while I prepare the pride for battle.'

Battle? Zana thought.

Ramina must have seen his confusion.

'There are things I will teach you, Zana—not now but later. There is, however, one thing you must know. Many centuries ago, a djinni freed the first pride of manticores from their creator, a magus looking to create the perfect soldier for her emperor. Since then, the manticores have owed a debt of gratitude to the djinn. Vul foresaw how you'd need our help, Zana. And he also saw how you'd present us with the perfect opportunity to repay the debt we owe the djinn.'

16

With the sun overhead, the four giant golems, one of them built that morning, advanced on the city. Three of them wielded hammers, while a fourth carried what looked like a cauldron. Behind them, and twice the height of a djinni, marched twenty smaller golems. Mounted guardsmen, armed with spears and shields, and archers on foot followed the smaller golems.

Sweat trickled down Roshan's back. She'd insisted on remaining close to Navid and, if need be, raise a dome or a portal for him. Her bracelet channelled the emotions of the djinn who lined the battlements and stared past the crenellations. They sapped her of energy as they wrestled with their fears and prepared to face the imminent onslaught.

Archers ran around the advancing golem, halted and fired arrows just high enough and far enough to cover the ground between the golems and Baka's walls.

'They know we've set traps,' Navid said.

The giant golems marched on. The soldiers and smaller golems kept close to the arrows projecting from the ground.

'We have to fall back,' Navid said. 'It won't be long before they reach the city's doors.'

Below, the lead golem triggered a trap hidden beneath the sand. It broke a clay tablet inscribed with an incantation and imbued with Core power. The golem unwittingly raised a portal and fell through it. The second golem flung away its hammer, raised its arms and hurled itself over the portal, sending sand and dust billowing into the air.

Roshan watched as the contours of the golem widened and flattened to form a bridge over which the third giant strode. She raised a protective dome over herself and Navid, not sure if she could prevent iron arrowheads from penetrating it.

Across the bridge, the golem hefted its iron-headed hammer. Behind it, the archers knelt and raised their bows. The golem holding the cauldron, the cavalry and the smaller golems didn't cross the bridge.

'Hold your positions,' Emad cried.

The wall shook as the iron hammerhead passed through the protective dome and slammed against the door.

Roshan felt the ramparts judder.

Before the golem could raise its hammer for a second strike, three spear-like jets of yellow flame burst from the crenellations and struck the golem's legs. Three sets of three djinn continued to direct the flames, melting the golem and turning its legs to glass.

Unable to move, the golem twisted at the hips as it raised its hammer. Roshan and Navid leaned forward at the scream of rock and glass splintering. With its feet fused to the ground, its thighs shattered and sent the golem's torso toppling backwards, the hammer still gripped, the magic holding the golem together failed and its torso collapsed into a heap of sand.

A cheer went up along the battlements.

Too exhausted to shout, Roshan noticed how her brother remained silent. He pointed at how the golem carrying the huge cauldron in one hand now crossed the bridge.

'That's a crucible,' he said.

Roshan's legs shook.

A deep-red glow emanated from inside the crucible. Yellow flames danced and flickered across its shimmering surface. The golem lifted the crucible, one hand supporting the back. It rested its weight on its back foot and swung the crucible backwards.

'Retreat,' Emad yelled. 'Molten iron.'

Everyone positioned along and beneath the ramparts rushed to the stairs and the rope walkways. Some stopped to raise portals, which faltered due to the closeness of the iron, and then sped off again. Roshan raised a portal to the ziggurat, its edge orange and not azure.

'This way,' Navid yelled to the djinn. He looked up and his eyes bulged. Roshan followed his gaze.

A smouldering, impenetrable splatter-shaped cloud hung in the air. It sent sparks twisting and whizzing in all directions. The fiery cloud splashed onto the ramparts, setting them alight and filling the air with its ferrous tang.

Roshan's protective dome swelled and deflected some molten iron back over the crenellations. She allowed herself a short sigh of relief when she saw djinn heading towards her portal, her dome also protecting them. The iron, however, caused them to shuffle along like old men.

Emad was the last djinni to reach them.

'That's everyone,' he said, his words slurred. He disappeared into the portal.

The walls shook as something hard struck the door.

Navid turned to look over the battlement.

'Don't,' Roshan said, her throat dry. 'I can't hold this dome much longer.'

He helped her though the portal and onto the third tier of the ziggurat. Roshan looked behind and saw Navid arrive. The portal collapsed.

The third tier was an empty room large enough to hold two

hundred djinn. Stockpiled urns filled with water and sacks of rations filled one corner. Four windows, one on each wall and with a knee-high parapet, provided a sweeping view of the city.

Djinn lay on the floor, their clothes and skin burned by the iron. Some had passed out, while others cried out in agony. The cries stopped moments after Roshan wished the iron away. Not all the iron, however, disappeared.

Her auric energy was woefully low.

'You, you and you,' Emad said, pointing at three of the younger djinn. 'Send the injured to the ships.'

A ringing sound echoed off the walls below. Emad dashed to the west-facing window, several djinn close behind.

If she hadn't recognised the sound of the golem's hammer striking the city's doors, she would have sat down and fallen asleep.

'Help me,' she said to Navid.

She leaned on him and together, they moved as fast has her legs would let them.

'What's wrong?' Navid said. 'Are you hurt?'

She shook her head.

'I don't have much auric energy left,' she said. 'I just need to rest.'

A *clang* ran through the city.

She reached the window to see how the copper lining the lower half of the left door had curled back on itself, the wood it had enclosed lying in splinters beneath it. Because of the iron, the dome surrounding the city and the symbols protecting the doors had failed.

The first to enter Baka were the smaller golems. Their steps broke the tablets buried under the sand. Clouds erupted around them and shaped themselves into war hounds.

The giant golem dropped its hammer and bent down, disappearing behind the wall.

'What's it doing?' Navid said.

Fingers appeared beneath the rent in the door and clasped it. A groan filled the air. A screech followed as the golem tore the door's massive lower hinge from the wall. The golem still held on to the door but didn't move.

What's it waiting for?

Mounted guardsmen rode through the gap the golem had made. Their iron spearheads made short work of the war hounds. A single touch from the spear and the mastiffs disintegrated into piles of sand.

'Evacuate the city,' Emad called. 'Everyone except the war council to leave for the ships—now! Wait there until further orders.'

Roshan understood Emad's reasoning. There had been little time to prepare, and what the djinn had prepared wasn't enough to stop the empire. That didn't make it easy to accept the fact they'd held the city for only a morning.

Below them, infantry galloped through the streets, their spears held out and shields close to their chests. Archers poured in and headed for the stairs leading to the ramparts.

She had to try—she'd promised herself she would after the second attack.

Roshan closed her eyes. There was no hesitation and no self-reproach over her next thought. Baka was alive. The king, her uncle, had chosen this place as the djinn's next home. If it meant they didn't have to keep running, and she could buy the djinn time to find out how to awaken Baka, she'd live with the consequences of what she was about to wish for—even if she ended up killing Yesfir and the other daevas.

I want all the guardsmen in Baka and in the high magus's encampment to return to Persepae.

Roshan opened her eyes and leaned a little more against her brother.

Down below, more infantry filled the streets and archers swarmed along the ramparts.

There was nothing left. She'd used up all of her auric energy. Roshan rubbed her face. She'd been an idiot. She should have made such a wish this morning, when she still had the energy.

'Hey?' Navid said.

Roshan hadn't realised she'd dug her fingernails into Navid's shoulder.

'Why did you do that?'

'I've run out of auric energy. I just tried to wish the guardsmen away, but nothing happened.'

Navid hugged her, forcing her to blink back tears.

'Take off your bracelet,' he said.

She saw Shephatiah step out of a portal and approach Emad.

'We've evacuated the city,' he said.

'Council members, to your positions,' Emad called.

With Navid's help, Roshan turned around. Including Emad, only five djinn remained in the room. One of them was Behrouz. All five rushed to the north-facing window.

'Come on,' she said.

Her brother frowned.

'Your bracelet. Whatever they'll do, they must do it with what's left of their own energy. For now, you can't help them.'

Although she wanted to keep it on, Navid was right. She slipped the bracelet off and dropped it into her tunic's pocket.

Navid led her to the window. Her steps felt lighter and less draining.

Water spilled through a portal in the square below. Before it hit the ground, the water spun to create four separate vortices.

'Increase their rotation before you send your stream into the city,' Emad said, his forehead beaded with sweat. 'It has to be the force of the water and not our magic that hits those soldiers. If there's too many soldiers with iron shields, direct the water at a building's walls and bring it down on them.'

Roshan watched the water snake its way through Baka's streets. A vortex struck a wall and rebounded against a retreating infantryman, sending rider and horse on a collision course with the one behind them.

Such resistance until the end was admirable but pointless. They'd lost the city. What was the point of fighting? They needed to leave.

A loud crash came from her left.

The golem had pulled the left door off its remaining hinge. It entered the city with one broad sweeping step and brought down a line of animal stalls with a single kick.

Roshan slipped her arm from her brother's shoulder and sat down cross-legged. Navid didn't object.

Baka was done for. The war council would realise that soon enough. Until then, she might as well close her eyes and surrender to exhaustion.

17

---

oshan rose above the city and drifted until she hovered halfway between Baka and the encampment. From where she floated, she saw how the dome protecting the city had collapsed.

Guardsmen, mounted and on foot, streamed across the golem bridge and into the city. A long clang rang out. To her right, the golem who'd reduced one of Baka's doors to splinters and crumpled copper now used its hammer to batter the ziggurat. The dome surrounding it failed to prevent the iron hammerhead from striking the building. Part of its wall caved in.

Other than her father, her brother, Behrouz and three other djinn, no one else remained to defend the city.

Roshan recalled the two triremes anchored at sea. She rose a little higher before being buffeted by a breeze and sent eastward. Two men and a woman stood on the eastern ramparts. They wore the white tunics and leggings of magi and stood over a glowing symbol they'd carved into the battlement's brickwork. They chanted an incantation and waved their hands over the symbol. Farther eastward, out to sea, another giant golem, this one made from the beach's pebbles, rocks and boulders, waded through the water and towards the ships. Last night, Emad had ordered all the djinn's children be moved to one of the triremes. She remembered the narrow alleyway in Arshak and poor Daniyel. If she didn't do something, and do it quickly, the children on the trireme would suffer the boy's fate.

Roshan hung in mid-air, unable to decide whom to help first: those in the ziggurat or the children out at sea?

Roshan made a swift, painful choice. She raised an orange-rimmed portal with a thought. She had to save the children and the rest of the djinn evacuated to the ships.

'That's the wrong choice.'

Roshan turned and found herself standing on the sand between the encampment and the city. She faced Manah. The lamassu pointed with his chin at the encampment.

'That's where you should go. The only way for all of this to end is to kill Sassan. Your power has faded. Use what's left to stop Sassan and put an end to his madness.'

She glanced back at the ziggurat and saw a dust devil. The debris from the city's destruction appeared and disappeared behind the swirling column of sand. It bumped against the golem hammering the ziggurat and tore a chunk from its back. Within a few heartbeats, the gap the dust devil had made refilled with sand.

The golem ignored the whirlwind and struck the ziggurat's third tier with a blow that cut through a section. The tier collapsed, spilling over the sides of the building. In the same moment, the dust devil stopped revolving. Sand and debris spilled into the city, billowing dust and burying her brother, father and Behrouz.

Roshan's bracelet burned and then turn icy cold.

The children, the others on the second ship.

Manah remained impassive, unaffected by the death and destruction. Roshan curled her hands into fists.

'Don't take your anger out on me,' Manah said. 'You should

be angry with yourself. The fall of Baka and the end of the djinn are your fault. You've been passive for fear of hurting the djinn.' Manah surveyed the city, its ziggurat obliterated. 'It's ironic, don't you think, that by doing nothing to avoid harming the djinn, you killed them.'

Roshan touched her bracelet and felt nothing. They were all dead.

Roshan's fell to her knees. She looked up. Manah had gone. The giant golem stood immobile over the spot on which the ziggurat had stood.

From behind her came the rattle of chains. Looking over her shoulder, she saw a shackled woman approach. Exhausted, Roshan pushed herself up. It took a while to recognise Yesfir's face beneath the swellings, bruises and cuts.

'You're dreaming,' Yesfir said through puffy lips. She pointed at Baka with manacled hands. 'But all this will become real if you don't wake up.'

18

Roshan woke to the sound of cheering. She rubbed her eyes, reached into her tunic's pocket and touched her bracelet. Across from her, Navid and the five djinn stared raptly out of the north-facing window. Navid and Emad had their arms on each other's shoulders as they pointed and cheered.

Although her tiredness hadn't entirely disappeared, she felt stronger and steadier on her feet. Roshan dragged herself over to the window as quickly as her stiff joints allowed. What she saw below caused her to cover her mouth.

From the sand heaped on roofs, inside courtyards and along streets and alleyways, Roshan assumed that hosing the city with seawater had undone all the golems. But that hadn't made her want to cheer. Manticores, huge manticores, ran down Baka's streets and across rooftops. The manticores dwarfed the guardsmen, whose heads barely reached their shoulders. Roshan saw a female manticore, up on a roof, impale an archer with its stinger, raise the thrashing guardsman into the air and fling him at a cavalryman below. Another used its tail as a club. Worse were the claws. A male manticore jumped from rooftop to rooftop as it chased a mounted guardsman on the street below. His horse clearing the street and entering the square beneath the ziggurat sealed the guardsman's fate. The manticore pounced and swiped as it passed over the fleeing horse and rider. The rider's torso flopped backwards onto his horse's croup and then slid off, while his legs remained attached to the saddle's stirrups.

Roshan turned away. Navid did too.

'I can't imagine our Zana becoming as large and as lethal as those manticores down there,' her brother said. 'Emad and I counted twenty-five of them. He's hoping more will come to our aid.'

Roshan had seen what Zana was capable of in Derbicca. It wasn't difficult to imagine that one day, he could slice a man in half with a single blow. No, what she found harder to accept was the high magus giving up now the djinn had allies.

Roshan glimpsed Shephatiah appear out of mid-air.

He announced himself with a 'Your Highness.'

Along with everyone else, she and Navid approached the djinni, eager to hear his report.

'Go ahead, lad; spit it out,' Emad said.

'I spotted six manticores running towards the enemy's camp.' Shephatiah glanced at Behrouz. 'One of them is Zana. So far, they've used the rocks to remain hidden. I could only see them from the top of the ziggurat. I don't think those watching from the encampment's tower will have seen them.'

Behrouz rubbed the back of his neck.

'He found the pride,' he said. 'Zana said he would rescue Yesfir.' He shook his head, his eyes wet. 'The boy's keeping his word.'

Shephatiah looked from Behrouz to Emad. He hadn't finished. Emad nodded for him to continue.

'Another golem is being built. Its feet, ankles and calves are visible. And there are more riders heading our way.'

Everyone absorbed the news with bowed heads.

Circles rimmed the djinn's eyes, and the flames surrounding their irises were mostly orange. Emad's were yellow. As if they'd prematurely aged, their complexions had turned pallid.

What are they going to do when that giant golem is complete? Unless the manticores withdrew from the city, they wouldn't be able use water to hold back the troops and the golem. My auric energy's gone. What do they hope to achieve by defending the city?

'Roshan.'

Emad studied her through narrow eyes.

'What are you thinking?'

Unsure how he'd react to the truth, she hesitated, until she remembered some of what the manacled Yesfir had said.

...all this will become real...

'Manah visited me while I slept,' she said, then told everyone about her dream. When she'd finished, she said, 'All this won't stop until we put an end to Sassan.'

The coldness in her voice, the matter-of-factness of her words shocked her. The high magus had to die. She then volunteered herself to do it.

'Absolutely not,' Emad said. 'You look shattered. It's best we head for the ships and leave.'

Before she could reply, Navid spoke.

'Everyone's shattered,' he said. 'I hate to admit it, but Roshan's right. I don't know how far you intend sailing those ships, because, as I understand it, the seal has a long reach. Once he knows how to use it, what's there to stop the high magus from summoning the djinn from wherever they're hiding? You can't keep running. We need to take back the seal, even if it means killing High Magus Sassan.'

Emad scratched his chin.

'I agree.' He sighed. 'But that doesn't mean I like your proposal.' He tapped his bracelet. 'Taking it off, Roshan, was a good idea. Here and on the ships, we're all spent. I think we have enough auric energy left for one more assault. With Sassan here, so close to Baka, we have to attack when he least expects it.' He gazed up at the ceiling. 'Unless Armaiti is watching us.' He pointed at himself and then two others. 'I, Shephatiah and Rabbu will stay here and keep the high magus and his general busy.' He nodded at Roshan. 'You and Behrouz find a way to take the seal from Sassan.' He faced Navid. 'Go with your sister. It's my hope that, compared to the rest of us, you're immune to the seal. If anyone can take that ring from him, it's you.' Emad then faced Shephatiah. 'Go down and get a manticore's attention. Tell her what we're going to do. Tell her the manticores must stay on the roofs.' He touched his forehead. 'And tell them I said thank you.' He waved his hand. 'All right, let's get ready.'

Roshan glanced at her brother. Had her suggestion just sent everyone to their deaths?

'I know,' Navid said. 'This probably won't work. But things are desperate. We have to try.' He held out his arms.

She stepped into his hug.

'Roshan, Navid.'

Emad approached, his brow furrowed.

'I don't like this one bit,' he said. He bowed his head and paused. 'In the last few days, I've lost Aeshma and my brother. For all our sakes, please come back. As a djinni trying to save his people, I want you to go, and I want you to save us. But understand that letting you go is the hardest decision I've ever made.'

Navid was the first to embrace him. Roshan joined them.

They untangled themselves at the same time Behrouz arrived.

Emad craned his neck.

'Promise me you'll take care of these two and you'll bring back my niece.'

'I will,' Behrouz said.

Emad traced an arc between the three with his index finger.

'If it's too dangerous, come back. Don't get captured and be used against the djinn. Return here, or else meet us on the ships. Got that?'

Roshan, Navid and Behrouz nodded.

She slipped her bracelet back on. Roshan didn't plan on channelling auric energy to the djinn. Through it, she could feel Emad's presence and the other djinn. The sensation galvanised her. At the first sign of danger, she'd take it off. For now, she needed to feel all those lives, needed to know there was a reason to fight the fear making her legs tremble. If conserving her auric energy wasn't enough to help her confront Sassan, she had another way—a more drastic way—to renew her energy.

19

Sassan's heart sank at the view from the platform.

Guardsmen, their boots pounding the wooden steps, rushed up and down, carrying either reports from the front line or new orders issued by General Afacan and two of his senior officers.

Below and to his left, twelve magi, double the number required, worked on the new golem's construction. Even with twelve of them, only the golem's feet, ankles and calves protruded from the sand. They were taking too long. Sassan fought the urge to shout at them to hurry. He glanced to his right.

The general appeared untroubled by the manticores. Their appearance and the reports of them killing guardsmen complicated Sassan's life. The manticores were a private race who hadn't involved themselves in empire affairs—until now. The emperor wouldn't be happy when he heard how Sassan had made him a new enemy.

Sassan braced himself, then gripped the railing. The tower swayed as if the nails holding it together had come loose.

Why, he wondered, *have you brought me this far, God, if you're going to abandon me and let victory slip from my grasp? Why didn't you warn me about the manticores? Are you unhappy with me?*

The question made him want to break something. He'd done everything God expected of him, endured unbearable pain which had left him unable to think clearly for more than an hour without another dose of poppy juice. The reports coming in described how streams of water gushing from a portal had swept back the small golems, the large golem and the guardsmen. And then the manticores had appeared inside Baka and massacred the survivors.

'General,' he said, 'what are you doing about those manticores?'

The general turned from his officers.

'I'm about to order more archers into the city. Under protection from cavalry, they'll make their way up to the ramparts. From there, they'll be high enough to be out of the manticores' reach.'

It sounded like a good plan. Sassan glanced at the bow he kept close by. And if the female djinni turned up, he'd shoot her with the sabaoth's arrow.

'Very good,' Sassan said. 'It won't be long before the golem is ready.'

The general's brow bunched.

'There's no need for another, High Magus. Without your golems, we would never have made it inside Baka. The men are fighting hand-to-hand. The smaller golems could help by distracting the manticores. For now, we don't need a larger one.'

Sassan's cheeks flushed. Was the general patronising him? He tightened his grip on the railing. If he let go, he'd stomp off and make himself look petulant. Should he need his help, the general would ask for it. Sassan needed to wait and pray to God for guidance. Baka wasn't theirs yet. After Baka had surrendered and he'd mastered the seal, the victory itself would be more important than how they'd taken the city.

Sassan let go of the railing and straightened. He had the sabaoth's arrow and the seal, each one proof enough he was God's chosen. The lack of poppy juice and the manticores' arrival soured his mood. God still guided him, and God needed him to relax.

Two columns of infantry trotted out from the camp, archers running between them. Once those men reached the ramparts, they'd make short work of the manticores, although it would take several arrows to stop each one.

Sassan thought he had his feelings under control when rows of red, blue and yellow winked on and off in front of his eyes. His undershirt stuck to his armpits and back, and Sassan's palms turned sweaty. He shuffled back from the railing as the colours brightened and the seizure claimed him.

'General—' he managed, before the convulsion swept the world from under his feet and he blacked out.

Sassan opened his eyes and found himself standing just beyond the cordon of guardsmen surrounding the encampment. The eagle-headed spirit stood next to him, its wings spread, hiding his own shadow behind them.

The spirit wrapped its arm around his waist, and Sassan gasped as it lifted him into the air. His body slipped a little in its grip.

This is a vision, *he told himself.* You won't fall.

They rose higher. His side pressed against the spirit's as it banked to its right and towards a line of jagged outcrops. There was no need to fly over them to see the six manticores, a pair of them much smaller than the others. They all streaked towards the encampment.

A hundred paces farther down from them, three djinn stepped out of a portal, bringing the manticores to a halt. One of them was the young female djinni who'd appeared in his dream.

The view below rippled, and he stood again inside the encampment where the djinni and the daevas were being held. The spirit pointed. Sassan followed its taloned finger. The three djinn and the manticores passed down a corridor of tents and entered the area he'd arrived in.

Now that he understood the purpose of the vision, Sassan turned to thank the eagle-headed spirit but found it had gone.

The young female djinni was coming to him.

Armed with the knowledge and confident that once she was dead, the djinn would offer no resistance to his commands, Sassan woke.

General Afacan knelt over him. He tried to rise. The general pressed down on his chest.

'You're not well, High Magus,' he said. 'You were carried you down from the tower.'

Sassan shook his head. His lips stretched into a grin.

'I've never felt better, General.' He pushed the general's hand away and sat up. 'I had a vision. We can expect some visitors quite soon. If they're to receive a proper reception, we must hurry.'

20

Roshan's portal stopped short of the six manticores, all of whom slid to a stop.

'Father!' Zana cried. He ran into Behrouz's arms.

Roshan swallowed while djinni and manticore embraced. Behind them, the five manticores, three females and two males, watched the reunion.

'They're even bigger close up,' Navid whispered.

She and her brother bent to share a hug with Zana, careful to avoid the quills beneath his short mane.

Zana made the introductions. The female who looked to be about Zana's age was Nahrian, and the two other females were Gula and Ri. The ebony-skinned male was Vul, and the other was Samdan. All five wore a white cross-shaped scar on their right shoulder.

'We saw you from the ziggurat,' Behrouz said.

Zana cast a wary eye at Behrouz.

'And you're here to help us rescue Mother?' he said.

From the way the manticores regarded them, Roshan got the impression they weren't looking for permission to rescue Yesfir. They needed to word their answer carefully.

'Emad has evacuated Baka,' she said. 'We're going to stop the high magus so that the djinn won't have to keep running. Since there are others in the camp, including Yesfir, we'll rescue them, too. If it helps, I can raise a portal that will open behind the encampment.' She glanced from Zana to the adult manticores. 'Would that be acceptable?'

Without deliberating, Ri nodded.

'It is,' she said. 'Vul will go with you. There are many guardsmen and you will need help.'

Behrouz thanked her. He faced Zana and said, 'As soon as you've found Yesfir and the others, let me know and I'll raise a portal to Emad's ship.'

Roshan raised a portal big enough to accommodate the manticores. She had to lock her knees to prevent herself from falling. Ri stepped through the portal. Gula, Nahrian and Samdan followed. Before he stepped through, Zana looked back at the four of them. He gave a determined nod before he disappeared.

'Zana's scared,' Behrouz said. 'He hid it well, but I could tell.'

Roshan collapsed the portal and raised a second, one that opened beneath the tower. Her skin had turned clammy, and her light-headedness meant she had to squat while she waited for them to enter the portal. Navid frowned at her.

Keep going, she told herself. *Think of the children on the ship.*

'It's nothing,' she said to Navid. 'I just need to get my breath back.'

He shook his head.

'Stay here.'

To lie down and sleep for an hour was tempting.

She rose and gave Navid a weak shove before he could complain.

Inside the encampment, Vul had already whipped, battered and clawed his way through the cordon of guardsmen blocking their way.

A golem twice Navid's size charged them.

Behrouz recited an incantation. A knife appeared in his hand. Roshan blinked, and someone cried out. Behind the golem and close to the tower, a magus fell, hands clutching his chest and the knife's hilt jutting from it.

Behrouz punched through the immobile golem, returning it to dust and sand.

Roshan raised her arms, her hands framing the tower ahead of her. About to recite an incantation, she shook her head. She imagined her hands enclosing the tower and clapped.

The edges of the tower fractured first, and its middle section disintegrated a heartbeat later. The men on top, three of them dressed in the black leggings and tunic of a guardsman and the other in a magus's all-white, fell. None of them landed well.

Roshan's legs gave way, and she landed on her bottom.

While Vul continued to tear into the guardsmen with his stinger and claws, Navid pulled her up. Her arm draped across his shoulder, they joined Behrouz, who stood over the remains of the tower. He gripped a scimitar.

'Is that him?' she said when they reached the fallen magus.

Already exhausted, Roshan wanted to collapse when she saw the magus's glassy stare.

'No,' Navid said. 'It isn't.'

Roshan looked up and yelped. Three guardsmen approached, their shields raised and spears levelled at them.

Behrouz took a backwards step.

'Iron,' he said, and groaned.

A stinger pierced the middle guardsman's chest. It lifted him screaming, making him a head taller than his comrades. Before the other guardsmen could turn, Ri batted them out of the camp —one towards Baka and the other beyond the encampment. With an expert flick of her tail, Ri hurled the impaled guardsmen into the air.

Nahrian appeared in front of the older lioness. Blood smeared her mouth and her eyes shone with excitement.

'Zana's found his mother,' she said.

Behrouz stepped past Roshan and knelt before Nahrian.

'Where?'

Nahrian half-turned. She looked eager to return to where she'd come from.

'Come with me. I'll show you.'

Behrouz stood and faced the twins.

Navid's grip on Roshan's shoulder tightened.

'It's a trap,' Navid said. He pointed at the dead magus. 'It's like before; they're expecting us.'

Behrouz shrank at Navid's reminder.

'You're probably right, but I have to try,' he said. He slipped his bracelet off and put it in his tunic's pocket. 'You two should continue looking for the high magus.'

Roshan recalled the events of two nights earlier.

'If it's a trap,' she said, 'the high magus and the seal will be at the centre of it.'

Navid's grip hadn't loosened.

'I don't like this,' he said.

Neither do I, Roshan thought.

'Change into a rat,' she said. 'I'll carry you until we reach Zana. Then hide. If it is a trap, there's still a chance you can save us.'

Navid squinted at her, and the bridge of his nose crinkled.

'Are you mad? You can hardly stand.'

'I'll carry her.'

The voice belonged to the lion, Vul, who stood behind her. His gaze flicked from Navid to Roshan.

'I'll shift. You're too weak to hold on to my mane.'

Calls came from behind the tents. On her left, spearheads bobbed towards them.

'Do as I say, Navid. We have to go.'

Her brother scowled at her before disappearing beneath a cloud. She bent down so Navid could run up her arm, then gasped when arms scooped her up. She tilted her head to see Vul appraising her, his broad shoulders bare.

He's naked.

Navid laughed as Vul followed behind Nahrian and Behrouz, the lioness Ri clearing a path.

'At a time like this, my sister's embarrassed,' Navid said.

Too exhausted to argue, she closed her eyes and rested her cheek against Vul's chest.

'WAKE UP,' Navid said. 'You need to put me down.'

Roshan opened her eyes and had to remind herself where she was. She told Vul to stop.

His forearm slid from beneath her knees as he planted her back on her feet.

'Thank you,' she said, without looking back.

Roshan counted a dozen daevas, their faces grey and their eyes red-rimmed from having to wear iron for so long. They stood huddled together between two tents, the flaps pulled back to reveal their emptiness. Manacles lay in a heap and to one side. The lioness Gula, naked and human, bent over an unconscious daeva and removed the pins from his manacles. Samdan, the lion and still a manticore, stood guard.

'Remember what we agreed,' Navid said.

She put him down. Navid scampered over to one of the empty tents and burrowed beneath it.

Roshan stepped forward. She raised her hands and dropped them. It took less effort to think a portal to the ships than raising one with Core power.

The orange-edged portal appeared a blink later.

'Go,' she said to the daevas. No one had moved. 'Prince Emad is waiting for you,' she added.

Her father's name spurred them into action. Gula carried the unconscious daeva to the portal. Two of the daevas took him from her and passed through.

Dizziness made it hard to stand.

'Where are the others?' Navid said.

Before she could answer, a familiar voice called her name.

'Roshan—hurry.'

The call came from ahead of her and belonged to Behrouz. Until that moment, Roshan hadn't noticed Behrouz's and Zana's absence.

Once all the daevas had departed, the portal collapsed.

Again, without warning, Vul swept her up.

Ri bounded forward. Vul turned. Gula had shifted back into a manticore.

'I'll be right behind you,' Gula said.

Vul nodded. He sprang forward to catch up with Ri.

Roshan squeezed her eyes shut against the rising dizziness. At the back of her mind, the lack of resistance they'd encountered on their way to and during the daevas' rescue confirmed Navid's suspicion: they were running into an ambush.

'Don't let them see you,' she told her brother.

They entered a clearing surrounded by tents. There was no sign of guardsmen.

Vul slowed to a halt. Up ahead, Roshan saw Behrouz with his back to her. A little to one side of him, far enough for Roshan to see part of her face, stood Yesfir. Neither djinni moved, spoke or reacted to their arrival.

So, this was the trap. Both djinn were likely under the seal's influence. The high magus had to be nearby. The only way for her to draw him out was to take the bait.

'Put me down, please, Vul,' she said.

Her feet touched the ground, making her wobble.

She knew she was spent. In her current state, she wasn't a threat to anyone. She had remained conscious only because she'd stopped channelling auric energy. Roshan had hoped for a swifter recovery. Now she'd have to rely on the contingency plan she'd thought up before leaving Baka.

'That's not a plan,' her brother said. 'It's a gamble.'

She straightened at the sound of Navid's voice. No sooner had she conceived the plan, she'd hidden it. She knew Navid would have protested. And if he knew it, if they'd discussed it previously, she'd have increased the chances of Armaiti hearing it, too.

'I would have asked you to help me with this, Navid,' she said. 'But for now, stay out of harm's way until I need you.'

Roshan closed her mind to Navid's voice, then turned to Vul.

'I have to reach Behrouz,' she said. 'I'd need you to accompany me.' Vul canted his head and raised an eyebrow.

'We've walked into a trap, but I think I can turn it to our advantage. When we're halfway, injure me. I planned on asking my brother to break my arm. I wasn't sure he could, but you could do it easily. If I don't start walking now, I'll pass out.'

She managed a step and then another. Vul placed a supportive arm around her.

'Thanks,' she said, her voice a whisper.

Each step required a supreme effort. Roshan reminded herself of Yesfir sacrificing her auric energy to heal the wound she'd sustained inside Persepae's chancery. She thought of the inquisitive little boy, Ehsan, who'd surrendered his auric energy to Fiqitush before he and his family left for Baka. And then she remembered how Fiqitush had kept a watchful eye on her and Navid.

Halfway to Behrouz and Yesfir, Vul moved so fast, Roshan didn't know what he'd done until she saw her hand and wrist hanging from the middle of her forearm at a right angle.

She'd expected pain. She only felt the bones slide against

each other as she cradled her broken left forearm. The sensation made her gag. Roshan ignored the sour taste in her mouth.

'Go,' she said to Vul. 'Find Zana.'

She slid her feet two steps before her vision clouded. Up ahead, Behrouz and Yesfir hadn't moved.

'Roshan, what are you doing?' Navid cried, his voice filling her mind.

Roshan sank down to one knee, the throb from her broken forearm filling her body. She listed between consciousness and unconsciousness. The ground in front of her darkened. The cloudiness, however, had disappeared.

She looked up. Behrouz loomed over her.

'It's working,' she said, and smiled.

Behrouz either hadn't heard her or ignored her. He raised his hand, until it was shoulder-high, and struck her.

21

Water gushed through the streets below, driving back horses and soldiers and flattening the heaps of sand that were once golems. Manticores stood or sat on rooftops. They watched the empire's debris float past, waiting for the water to subside.

'Your Highness,' Shephatiah said.

Emad heard concern behind the words.

'What is it, lad?'

Shephatiah pointed at his own eyes, then nodded at Emad.

Emad saw how the flames around the youth's irises remained orange. He ground his teeth when he understood what the lad had tried to tell him.

'Have they gone out?' he said. He couldn't bring himself to say *Am I a daeva again?*

Shephatiah shook his head.

'They've turned yellow.'

Emad looked across at the other djinni, Rabbu, five decades older than Shephatiah. The flames circling Rabbu's irises were also yellow. Between them, it might be possible to soak the city one last time. His memory of standing outside Derbicca, Aeshma beside him, and the lack of auric energy to maintain a protective dome made him change his mind.

'We must conserve what energy we have left for helping the ships escape,' he said. 'There's no one left in Baka. It's time to go.' He nodded at both djinn. 'Go down and tell the manticores we're leaving. Please tell them they have my thanks and the djinn's thanks for all their help.' He raised a hand before they left. 'Once you're done, head for a ship. I'll stay behind and wait in case those in the encampment don't see the beacon and return here.'

Shephatiah raised a portal to the steps below. Rabbu left first.

'Good luck, Your Highness,' Shephatiah said, and stepped through.

Emad thought, *I'll have to speak with the lad about this* Your Highness *business.*

Up on the third tier, the silence felt as if the city were condemning him for abandoning it.

Emad raised his forearm and touched his bracelet. He closed his eyes and concentrated when he found it hard to sense the others. Navid's constant shape-shifting meant he didn't always wear his bracelet. That might explain why he didn't sense his son. As for his daughter, his niece and her husband, there were only two reasons he couldn't sense them: either they all hid beneath a protective dome, or they were all dead.

He'd played no role in the twins' upbringing, but he was the one who'd sent them off into danger and possibly their deaths.

I can't even be a father, he thought. *Fiqitush was mad, thinking I could lead the djinn.*

Except for the fallen viewing tower, the encampment looked no different from the west-facing window. As if sensing victory, more guardsmen rode towards the city.

Baka and the djinn were finished. Fiqitush's dream was over before it had begun.

Emad made his way over to the stairs leading up to the fourth tier. The ships needed to leave now, before the zealot and his soldiers realised where everyone had disappeared.

Up on the ziggurat's topmost tier, Emad circled the shoulder-high pile of wood. A sulphurous smell, lamp oil soaked up by the dry wood, filled the tier.

Emad checked his bracelet. Still nothing.

Tears of anger and frustration wet his cheeks. One man's zealousness had brought an entire nation to its knees, while God and a sabaoth had ensured the djinn never recovered from Solomon and the seal. Loss soon replaced the anger. He'd lost everything. First, his childlike cousin and then his brother—both within days of each other. And now the high magus had taken his niece and his children—Shafira's twins—from him. He rubbed away tears with the sleeve of his tunic.

Now isn't the time to mourn, he said to himself. *There's still work to do.*

Emad held out a hand, ready to recite the incantation to start a fire. Out at sea, once they saw the lit beacon, the two triremes would weigh anchor and row. They were to head north, hug the shoreline until it ran out and turn westwards so land remained visible from the port bow.

Ahead, the manticores began to leave. They bounded up the stairs to the northern ramparts, vaulted the crenellations and disappeared as they rounded the corner where cliff met beach.

It had been unbelievably easy for the empire—for Sassan—to defeat the djinn. There had to be some way of striking back, landing a blow against the empire and—more importantly to Emad—the high magus.

'The djinn aren't sailors,' he said out loud. 'You can't leave them to figure things out on their own. They'll probably clash oars as soon as they start rowing.'

Back in Derbicca, he'd missed his chance to kill Sassan while Behrouz had exchanged sword blows with his general. With the djinn's departure, Sassan was bound to enter Baka and survey the city. It was desperate of Emad to think he could make a difference. He had no choice. Even if they sailed away, Sassan had the seal and the means of summoning back those who remained djinn.

Emad lit the beacon, took the stairs down to the square and waited under a dome of invisibility and silence. If the high magus didn't enter Baka within the hour, or if magic or iron protected him, Emad would leave knowing he'd tried to end the djinn's plight. Then he'd have to hope Tarana's son, Zafran, and his band of mercenaries honoured their contract and killed the high magus.

22

Roshan heard a command.

'Wake up.'

Her eyes opened. The outline of a man stood over her, his features fuzzy. A couple stood opposite him, but they looked ahead instead of at her.

Roshan blinked to clear her vision. The trio were Behrouz, Yesfir and, holding a bow and a golden arrow, High Magus Sassan. Right then, she knew she should have felt more than relaxed detachment. She must have fallen clutching her broken arm, because she still held it. Thanks to Domain power, it had healed.

She glanced past them, left and then right. On her right, twenty paces away, stood a row of six manticores. They ignored the guardsmen fencing them in with spears. She glimpsed their faces. Zana sat on his haunches, his paws raised. Vul also raised his arms, his hands, palms up, level with his shoulders.

On her right stood guardsmen. Like Zana and Vul, some of them raised their hands, their palms facing her. At their centre stood a guardsman she remembered from Derbicca and Emad's rescue. He had traded sword blows with Behrouz while protecting the high magus.

A protective dome—you're inside a protective dome.

'If you try anything,' the high magus said, 'I'll command your friends here to kill you.'

He gestured at Yesfir and Behrouz, neither of whom moved.

The threat didn't affect her calmness. Instead, she noticed how the high magus swayed as he stared at her. Behind his gaze of curiosity she recognised a hunger she'd seen only during her days as a novice.

He craves poppy juice.

How had this small, drug-addled man caused the djinn and daevas so much suffering?

'You killed a man with a scream,' the high magus continued. 'But your eyes, they aren't like a djinni's.' He pointed the golden arrow at her. 'I should kill you. But if you do as I say, follow my commands, like these two'—he nodded at Yesfir and Behrouz —'I'll let you live. Under my command, you and the djinn will achieve many things and bring greater glory to God.'

She felt it then, the seal's influence. Just like two nights ago, it pushed at her will, attempted to drive it down into herself.

Laughter came from ahead of her. Roshan raised her head.

'Stupid girl,' Manah, the lamassu, said.

Manah's bearded face blurred. His beard disappeared. Manah's cheekbones grew more prominent and his bottom lip swelled in the middle. His altered features turned the sabaoth's face from male to female. His wing remained, but now the bull's body morphed into a human's, its contours female.

Roshan tensed her stomach and sat up. She clutched her healed forearm and glanced up at the high magus. Sassan continued to stare at her and not the sabaoth. He hadn't heard or seen the lamassu transform itself into a winged woman.

Armaiti?

'It is,' she said.

So, Manah was...

Roshan paused. Over the past three days, the lamassu who'd visited her in Iram and in her dreams wasn't Armaiti's nemesis; it was Armaiti herself. The sabaoth had called her a stupid girl, and she was right.

Armaiti's nose elongated and curved until it resembled a beak.

'You see it?' the high magus said. 'You can see the eagle-headed spirit God sends me.'

Before she could reply, the high magus stepped back from Roshan. In the space between them, close to the high magus's toes, letters as long as her hand appeared in the sand.

'Kill her,' they read.

The high magus's mouth worked. Roshan couldn't tell if he gasped for air or tried to speak. He flung aside his bow, grasped the golden arrow with both hands and raised it as if it were a spear.

'No, High Magus.'

Roshan turned her head. The guardsman she recognised called out to Sassan.

'She is our prisoner,' he continued. 'This not how a high magus behaves. What you're about to do is murder. Stop this at once. Otherwise, I'll arrest you and have you taken back to Persepae in chains.'

The high magus's turmoil reminded her of Manah's—or, rather, Armaiti's—exercises in the basin filled with stone columns. Armaiti had caused her to doubt herself, leaving her troubled about what to do. Roshan channelling her auric energy had helped the djinn, but its real purpose was to weaken her. And it had. At least some of what Armaiti-Manah had said was the truth. Domain power had healed her broken arm and replenished her aura. But what now? If she attempted to kill the high magus, would Armaiti intervene?

Roshan drew herself up and knelt on one knee. Armaiti had made a fool of her. Now she'd do the same to her.

'Command me, High Magus,' she said. Roshan continued to support her forearm.

The high magus looked over his shoulder at Baka. One hand released the arrow so he could point at the ziggurat.

'Put that out,' he said, referring to the fire burning on the fourth tier.

Again, the seal fought to displace her will. The pressure it exerted was an itch—an itch she could ignore.

Am I getting stronger?

Was her auric energy still being renewed?

She decided against standing for now. So long as the high magus thought he had the upper hand, she'd have the advantage of surprise.

Neither Yesfir nor Behrouz moved. Roshan felt Yesfir's presence at her side. Two nights earlier, when she'd rescued the three of them—Roshan, Behrouz and Navid—Yesfir hadn't hesitated. She'd accepted that others, daevas included, might get hurt.

Roshan looked past the high magus.

Stop burning.

The beacon winked out.

With the high magus's back to her, Roshan made to rise, wanting to see the look on Sassan's face when she wished him dead.

'What's that?'

Roshan remained kneeling and looked past Sassan's golden arrow.

Navid!

Behind the high magus, her brother, still a rat, burrowed into the sand, hoping he could get under the protective dome.

The high magus turned and looked down at her, his body swaying.

'Yesfir told me your brother can shape-shift,' he said. 'I command you to kill him.'

Roshan stopped holding her forearm and stood.

'KILL HER.'

Armaiti's yell shook the ground. The high magus held his arms out to stop himself from falling.

'Hold her,' he shouted. Sassan gripped the arrow and raised it above his head.

Behrouz grabbed Roshan from behind and held her upper arms with a crushing grip.

Yesfir, Behrouz and Navid, Roshan thought, *leave this protective dome.*

Against the background of Armaiti's laughter and the guardsman's loud protest, the high magus plunged the arrow into Roshan's chest. Behrouz had followed Roshan's command and let go of her. The force of the blow and the arrow lodging in her sternum drove her back down and onto one knee.

Dense, molten power poured into her. Neither Core power nor Domain power, this carried emotions, memories and knowledge—lost, ancient knowledge—that ran from the seal, down the sabaoth's arrow and through her body. It stopped at her right wrist and beneath her bracelet. Roshan's vision turned hazy. The power, the djinn's auric energy flooding into her, consumed her pain and yearned for release. Roshan closed her eyes and channelled the energy.

Not all the auric energy belonged to the djinn in Baka. Some of it wound its way back to those who'd lived for centuries, having forgotten their former lives.

A fisherman dropped the net he was about to cast. He dived from his boat into the sea, his legs forming a fish tail as he struck the water.

Up on a hilltop, a woman put her basket down and reached behind her to scratch an itch. Her fingers brushed feathers, wings, and the itch disappeared. She launched herself off the hilltop and took to the air.

A young shepherd trembled at the edge of a forest, his sling ready and his free hand filled with pebbles. Today, he meant to stop a lone wolf from taking his goats. The shepherd dropped the sling and pebbles to watch how fur coated his hands and his nails turned to claws. He howled his challenge and then charged into the forest.

The ground shook a second time, returning Roshan to the encampment.

'Let go of the arrow,' Armaiti shouted. 'She's draining the seal of its power.'

Roshan gripped the high magus's right wrist with both hands.

More ancient power flooded her body and then her mind.

She witnessed the fifteen nomadic djinn tribes and the days when they warred against one another. The power described their unification, the development of djinn magic and how formidable they'd become before the seal stripped them of their knowledge, memories and auric energy.

And now that power, having travelled through the sabaoth's arrow and into Roshan, returned to its people and made them whole again.

Roshan smiled.

Armaiti screamed.

'You can see it—can't you?' the high magus said. 'The eagle-headed spirit. God wants you dead.'

The pressure he exerted eased for a moment, and then he shoved with all his weight. The arrowhead passed through Roshan's sternum.

More power surged through her and turned her skin blue-grey. Whirls of orange rose to the surface.

'God never sent that spirit,' Roshan said. 'She used you to get to me.'

Flames erupted from her skin, and the high magus's tunic caught alight.

While the high magus thrashed and yelled for her to release him, she felt only the calm detachment she'd experienced when she'd woken. Domain power rushed through her like a torrent, burning muscle and sinew, drying bone. It didn't distress her that she burned at a rate too fast for her auric energy to heal her. This was Armaiti's plan all along. The sabaoth had gotten what she'd wanted, but Roshan had set the djinn free, and Emad could realise King Fiqitush's dream. That was all that mattered.

She looked away from the high magus who burned along with her, her hands fused to his wrists. To her right, Yesfir and Behrouz stood outside the dome. Yesfir pressed Navid—who hadn't shape-shifted—against her chest. From the way his tail twisted and swung, he struggled to free himself of her grip. She heard his mental anguish and experienced his shock and his confusion.

Blind now, she reached out to Navid with her mind.

'It's all right,' she said.

23

Emad sat beneath a dome of invisibility and silence. Seated a third of the way down the staircase from the ziggurat, he watched mounted soldiers scour the city for djinn. He resented how they rode around as if they owned Baka.

'You wouldn't look so smug if manticores still roamed the place,' he said to a passing rider. His resentment never made it past the dome.

Flakes of ash drifted around him and settled upon the foot of the stairs. A blackened twig, no longer than his little finger and not yet burned through, bounced once on the paving. Several more joined the twig.

Emad jumped up, flew down the stairs and ran into the middle of the square. He craned his head and groaned. The beacon had gone out.

'I'd wager a narwhal's tusk someone put it out,' he muttered.

By now, both ships would have weighed anchor and begun rowing.

'That's not the point,' he said. 'No one in the encampment knows about the ships. Why would they put the fire out?'

With little auric energy remaining, raising a window to check on the ships meant he might not have enough left to leave the city.

The city shook and interrupted the thought. His ankles and knees adjusted as Baka pitched. It was like standing on the deck of a ship. Emad had been a sailor for too long to feel seasick. Even so, he sat down before a sudden queasiness overwhelmed him.

Dizzy as though he'd drunk too much, Emad pressed down with his palms to steady himself. His skin prickled and turned clammy, and his saliva tasted bitter. As suddenly as it had struck him, the queasiness disappeared. He hauled himself up and, in case either the ground or he began to shake, he held out his arms for balance. The bitterness on his tongue remained and the concern he felt for the ships continued to weigh on him. Yet, somehow, he felt different. People, places and events, memories he couldn't be sure were his, tumbled into his head. Emad held up his hands. They looked the same, but when he clenched them, the surrounding air sizzled.

'Djinni!' a soldier yelled as he rode towards Emad, his short sword raised.

His disorientation must have caused his dome to collapse.

One half of him tensed to turn and run up the ziggurat's steps. The other half, the half alien to him, raised a hand. Emad spoke a single word. His mouth shaped and pronounced the word of power precisely.

What's a word of power? the half that wanted to run wondered.

Rider and mount flew into the air and over Baka's west-facing wall. The soldier's short sword clanged against the paving. Memories of brawls in inns where he often hurled his fellow drinkers over tables countered his surprise.

'I remember some of those fights,' he said, his recollection causing him to grin. They'd happened before Fiqitush had called him and the other djinn back. His grin dissolved. 'What have I done?' How much of his auric energy had he used up?

Emad noticed the soldier's fallen sword and stepped away from it.

The image of another sword—this one longer than the soldier's, curved and also made of iron—filled his mind. He'd won the sword from a Kemetian captain during a game of Ur. He'd worn that sword for years.

Emad shuffled towards the soldier's sword. The metal didn't cause his hand to recoil. Emad grasped the hilt, hefted the sword and tested its balance.

'I could touch and use iron just like humans,' he said. 'That was until Solomon arrived.'

He touched his bracelet. Still no Roshan. Did she have the seal? Had something happened to her because of it?

A rider swept past him but paid him no heed. A second rode by and did the same.

'What's going on?'

From among the riders, those farther ahead and closer to the city's crumpled door, came the call to retreat. Still gripping the sword, Emad turned and headed for a side street.

Halfway down, clogged and weighed down with silt and sand, he pulled off his sandals. Emad ignored the bodies, some hanging from the roofs of the single-storey buildings. He rounded a corner and found the mangled and torn bodies of their mounts, the sticky sand encasing parts of them.

His weight hadn't changed in the past two days. Back in Iram, he'd stopped to catch his breath after running only two hundred steps. Now, with wet sand sucking at his feet, he experienced neither breathlessness nor a sharp pain in his side. If not for the bodies in his path, he would have run even faster.

Emad reached the west-facing wall. Up ahead, a queue of soldiers, some nursing injuries, waited to pass through the gap left by the giant golem, who'd torn off a door. Riders and those on foot hesitated before stepping through the doorway. Rather than walk through it, it looked to Emad as if they jumped.

His bracelet warmed and pulsed with a rhythm Emad recognised. It compelled him to look up. Above him, Shephatiah's head poked over the ramparts. The young djinni gestured at him to come up.

'He should be on a ship, not here,' he said.

The stairs leading up were within ten steps of the retreating soldiers. It might be all right for the lad with orange flames and youth to raise portals here, there and everywhere, but Emad's auric energy was limited.

Emad regarded the sword he still grasped. Something had happened in the encampment. Otherwise, the soldiers wouldn't be retreating, and he wouldn't be holding an iron weapon as if it were bronze. Emad let the part he hadn't fully acquainted himself with raise the portal. He drew a circle with his finger, said the word of power and stepped through.

Shephatiah wasn't the only djinni up on the ramparts.

'Why aren't you lot aboard the ships?' Emad said.

Shephatiah's wide smile shortened and his brow bunched.

'Your Highness,' he said. He pointed to his eyes and then to Emad's. 'The seal's power has been released.'

Shephatiah spoke the truth. Instead of orange flames surrounding the lad's irises, bright-blue flames burned in their place.

The memories and the words of power, those were his old self, the parts the seal had torn from him.

'Come, Your Highness,' Shephatiah said, then directed him towards Baka's lone door.

The djinn Emad passed all possessed the same coloured flames.

'I thought I'd imagined it,' Shephatiah said. 'Those below had started rowing when we saw the beacon. Then the lookout said it had been extinguished. When I came up on deck, I couldn't believe what I saw. None of us could. When King Solomon used the seal, I and the others up here weren't born. The older djinn are'—Shephatiah searched for the right word—'confused by the things they're remembering. We don't have such memories, so we weren't affected.' Shephatiah pointed below and past the battlements. 'I couldn't believe what I'd seen from the ship.'

Horses and soldiers jumped to exit the city. Emad rubbed his eyes. Baka had risen by about the height of a man.

Fiqitush, you were right. Baka can fly.

'How did this happen, Your Highness?'

Emad shook his head.

'I don't know, and I have no memory of this city or any other that can do this. My guess is it's happened because the seal has returned our auric energy to us.' A thought crossed his mind. 'How did you raise a portal to get here?'

Shephatiah knitted his eyebrows.

'The usual way—why?'

So, the lad and the other youngsters didn't know about words of power. The seal had untainted the auric energy they'd inherited, which explained the blue flames. However, they hadn't been born until after Solomon had stolen both auric energy and memories from the djinn. Parents and the djinn elders passed down knowledge by word of mouth. The younger djinn would have to be taught how to weave magic with words of power, along with anything else Emad hadn't yet remembered.

'Don't worry,' he said. He checked his bracelet. Yesfir and Behrouz were safe. Emad swallowed. He gazed at Shephatiah. 'Return to the ships. I need fifty djinn.' He stared across the sand and past the single column of soldiers winding their way back to the encampment. 'I'm going to pay the high magus a visit.'

24

Armaiti watched as orange, smokeless flame consumed Roshan and Sassan. Both bodies had fallen back and onto their sides, their thin outlines within columns of flame. A moat of molten glass surrounded them.

Sassan's dome had collapsed the moment he'd lost consciousness. Yesfir, Behrouz, Navid, Zana and Vul watched from a distance. Fuelled by Domain power, the flames' intensity made it impossible for any of them to get closer than twenty paces.

Armaiti saw tears on most of their faces. Still in shock, Navid hadn't shape-shifted and remained a rat. He lay in the crook of Yesfir's arm. Vul's expression wasn't one of grief. With his brow creased and his lips pursed into a thin line, he looked more confused than upset. Armaiti guessed that none of them expected Roshan to die.

Armaiti smiled.

The seal's energy being transferred through the arrow and into Roshan had angered her. And the djinn on this world had caused her enough trouble. Her sentence, however, had ended. Any kind of retribution risked further punishment by the

Unmade Creator. She'd learned her lesson—she'd no longer interfere with Its creations.

General Afacan barked an order. The guardsmen behind the four manticores raised their spears, turned and marched towards the front of the camp, leaving this part of the encampment unguarded.

Armaiti caught Yesfir touching her bracelet. Behrouz did the same and then said something to Zana, who continued to cry. They all cast a final look at the bodies engulfed by flames. Yesfir wiped her eyes with the back of her hand. Navid sat frozen on her arm. She was the first to turn and leave. Behrouz, his face pale, was next. Zana followed him, which left only the naked Vul, who knelt, his eyes searching the flames. Intrigued by why he would be the last to leave, Armaiti touched his mind to read his thoughts. She discerned no emotions, thoughts or even a pulse. It was as if he didn't exist.

Vul's sister, Narian, called out to him. The other manticores had loped off. He rose, shifted and in one giant leap caught up with his sister.

Armaiti wiped sweat from her brow and felt slickness between her fingers.

Fingers?

She looked down and saw bare feet beneath her. A hard thumping came from inside her. Armaiti gasped for air, her shoulders rising and falling with each breath.

She closed her eyes to concentrate. Bright orange penetrated her eyelids. Back while Roshan knelt before Sassan, Armaiti had made herself visible to both of them—nothing more. If she remained incorporeal, she wouldn't feel the heat pressing against her skin. She wouldn't sweat.

Armaiti opened her eyes and found herself corporeal and human. Sunlight and flames seared her naked skin. Her legs gave out from under her. Armaiti ignored how the sand burned her shins and feet.

'She's dead,' she yelled at the sky. 'Free me.'

If she were being punished for Roshan's death, why hadn't the Unmade Creator warned her?

Her burning skin, her difficulty breathing and the hammering inside her chest all made it difficult to think. Was it possible the Unmade Creator had no intention of letting her leave this world?

It wanted Roshan dead, and she'd seen to it the girl had died. This couldn't be happening.

'You lied,' she shouted. 'You said You'd free me.' Tears came. 'Answer me. Please. Tell me what to do, but don't leave me here like this.'

Armaiti received no answer.

The heat grew unbearable.

She dashed towards the guardsmen's tents. This wasn't the first time she'd been corporeal. But those times were different. Back then, she'd used her thoughts to condense air particles into a solid shape of her design. This was different. As she moved, she felt the stretch and contraction of muscles and the tautness of ligaments. Her body quivered, tightened and ached regardless of her thoughts. It rebelled against her instructions. She thought so hard, her head throbbed and her eyes kept watering. Armaiti entered tent after tent, scattering belongings until she found what she was looking for.

The hunting knife's bronze blade was keen and oiled.

Armaiti pushed her head back and placed the knife's edge against her neck. She paused before lowering the blade. The knife then hung above the blue-green veins of her wrist. Armaiti gritted her teeth. Her clenched fist made her veins and tendons bulge. She willed her left hand to slide the blade down and across to sever the artery beneath. Other than shaking, her hand refused to move.

'I don't want to be like this,' she said.

She'd spoken the truth. So, why the need for self-preservation? Humans killed themselves all the time. Why couldn't she do it?

With both hands gripping the hilt, she tried to plunge the blade into her stomach. The blade's tip nicked the skin above her navel.

'You're no longer a sabaoth. You're powerless. You're not even a djinni. Why do you want to live?'

Armaiti dropped onto the edge of a cot. She held the knife above her foot and let go. Her foot moved before the knife buried its blade in the sand.

'You want to live because you're a coward,' she said, then buried her face in her hands.

The accusation depressed her. She was scared, scared because—unlike other humans—she knew what came after death. And now she was human, she couldn't face it.

An hour passed. Armaiti's breathing calmed and the thudding, her heart, slowed.

'I'm not ready to die,' she told herself.

Apart from her instinctive avoidance of death, she couldn't think why, given her circumstances, she wanted to live.

Armaiti scanned the tent, then plucked at a tunic and crumpled leggings. Both were stiff with dried sweat, the sour odour making her nostrils twitch. The garments matched her height, but they were baggy on her. The sandals she found had a broken strap. So long as she didn't run, their soles would prevent her own from burning. Armaiti retrieved the knife's sheath and tucked it into the belt holding up her leggings.

Outside, smoke curled up from the ashes of both fires. The moat of molten glass had solidified. Before she went marching off into the desert, she'd need water, lots. If she located a horse, could she master riding it?

Something glinted as she turned. Armaiti looked back at the heap of ash that had been Sassan. She shuffled forward to keep the sandal from sliding off her foot.

She didn't have to guess to know what it was. Power emanated from it, cooling the surrounding air. The power belonged to those djinn who'd died before the seal could return their auric energy to them. Armaiti squatted and blew the ash from the seal. To take it would mean her continuing to play the Unmade Creator's game, because everything that had happened until now was just that. If the Unmade Creator wanted to understand Its origins, she didn't see how her becoming human would help further that understanding.

Armaiti glanced at the sandal's broken strap. The clothes she'd stolen made her skin itch, and the tunic's muskiness made her heave. She pulled the hunting knife from its sheath and used it to fish the seal out from Sassan's remains.

She glanced over to her left and the mountains.

'I won't deny I'm scared,' she said, staring at the ring that hung from the knife's tip. It didn't matter whether the Unmade Creator heard her. 'And if I live as a human, it won't be as a hermit.'

She lifted the ring off the knife and held it between finger and thumb. The sun brightened, forcing Armaiti to squint.

'If it's a game You're playing, then I will play it. And while I play, I will taint this world. I will turn human against human and djinni against djinni until, one day, this world of Yours destroys itself.'

Armaiti slid the knife back into its sheath, then slipped the ring over her right index finger. The seal didn't fit, but that didn't stop some of the auric energy it contained from merging with hers. A word of power shrank the seal, and it fitted snuggly.

Armaiti's second word of power raised a portal.

25

Emad sat on the steps to the ziggurat, his mind thrumming with each new memory that surfaced. He'd almost forgotten his plan when Shephatiah stepped out of a portal. Behind him, other djinn appeared out of mid-air.

'While I was away,' Shephatiah said, 'some of the prisoners arrived on a ship.'

Emad touched his bracelet. His smile shrank when he couldn't detect Roshan and Navid. He turned to the assembled djinn.

'The empire's retreating, but there are still matters we need to settle.' A djinn, one of the younger ones he'd seen up on the ramparts, appeared and strode towards him. 'What is it?' he said, eager to leave for the encampment.

'Your Highness, there are three riders, soldiers, heading our way. Behind them are manticores and djinn.'

Emad nodded his thanks.

'I want five djinn to come with me. The rest of you, remain just outside the city and await further instructions.' He raised a portal halfway between Baka and the encampment. He ushered the five volunteers through it, Shephatiah being one. The remaining djinn raised their own portals, the older ones drawing a circle with a finger and voicing the word of power.

Outside Baka and able to make out the figures behind the three riders, Emad's apprehension grew. Several djinn rode manticores, including Behrouz and Yesfir. Alongside them strode a dozen djinn: former daevas captured in Arshak. There was no sign of the twins. Impatient for news, Emad marched out to meet them.

The riders drew up in front of Emad and dismounted. None of them carried a weapon. The middle rider waited for the soldier on his left to take his horse's reins. Emad recognised the man: first, outside Derbicca with Aeshma, and then inside the city, battling to protect the high magus from Behrouz.

The soldier approached. He raised an eyebrow in recognition.

'Emad,' he said, and performed a shallow bow. 'We've not been introduced. I am General Afacan.'

Emad nodded, then looked past the general. It would be a little longer for the manticores to reach them.

'Where's the high magus?' he said.

'That's why I'm here.' He gestured at the manticores and the approaching djinn. 'The high magus is dead. He died murdering a young woman, a djinni, I think.' He shook his head. 'I'm not sure what happened to him, but I'm sure the others will explain things better than I can.' The general stared down and to his right.

Roshan—it has to be her the bastard murdered. Emad felt his limbs shake. He scanned the group behind the general. *Where's Navid?*

'This pointless campaign is over,' the general said. He looked up. 'As soon as we've tended to the wounded, my men and I are returning to Persepae.'

Emad swallowed. He had to put the djinn's needs first. There'd be time soon enough for him to question the others and to grieve. He straightened and tried not to glare at the general.

'Tend to your wounded, General. When you're ready, I'll raise a portal to Persepae for them.'

Notches appeared in the general's brow.

Emad held a hand behind his back and clenched it.

'You humans have never tried to understand us. Send this message with your wounded to the emperor: leave the djinn alone, and the djinn will leave you alone.'

Again, the general gazed at the sand to his right.

'I will make sure he gets it, Emad,' he said, then looked up and sighed. 'All I can do is relay your message. Although I'm grateful for your help, I cannot guarantee how the emperor will react to it.' The general took a step forward and lowered his head. 'As a mark of respect,' he said, his voice low so only Emad heard him, 'please consider my advice: don't stay here for too long.' The general backed away, then said, 'I'll send a rider to let you know when our wounded are ready.'

Emad didn't move as he watched the general return to his horse, mount and ride away.

He was already crying when a bruised and battered Yesfir hugged him.

'Be careful,' she said, and pushed herself off him. 'You'll squash Navid.' She peeled back the top of her tunic's pocket. Inside, Navid lay curled in a ball. 'He was too shocked to shape-shift,' she said, her eyes teary. 'He watched her die—we all watched Roshan die.'

26

Emad joined Ramina and the eight other manticores who'd accompanied her to the city's doors. Behind them, Zana said his final goodbyes to Yesfir and Behrouz. The nine manticores, dressed in robes of white, had arrived an hour after dawn.

Three days had passed since the battle for Baka and the guardsmen's departure. Three days weren't enough for Yesfir to recover from her time with Sassan and to grieve for her father. And now Zana was leaving. Why couldn't the manticores have waited a little longer before holding young Zana to his promise? Ramina escorting Zana to the den of the Cross Scar pride reflected how seriously the manticores took a promise, even from a thirteen-year-old. Emad bent his head back and addressed the pride's leader.

'I didn't get to thank you personally for helping us,' he said. 'Your warriors bought us time to evacuate the city. Your intervention saved many lives.'

Ramina dipped her head.

'You're welcome, Emad.' Ramina bent forward, her gaze earnest. 'What next for the djinn and Baka?'

Emad scratched his chin. He had searched his brother's tablet for an answer to the same question.

'I'm not sure,' he said. 'It's as if Baka woke with the return of our auric energy. Since it stopped levitating, I can't shake the feeling it's waiting for something. Until I can discover what it is, Baka isn't going anywhere.'

Ramina's gaze remained sober. The significance of what he'd said wasn't clear enough.

'By now, the emperor will have received my message,' Emad continued. 'The djinn will leave the empire alone if the empire does the same. I don't know if the emperor will consider my message a request or a threat and how he'll react to either. I don't want to wait around to find out.' Like Ramina, Emad leaned forward. 'It's likely the general will include your helping us in his report. If he doesn't come after us, the emperor might come after the manticores.'

Ramina's grave expression didn't change.

'Let him come,' she said. Then, one side of her mouth curled upward. 'He must find us first. It can be treacherous, searching for a manticore's den.'

Emad had seen a guardsman torn in two by a manticore. Would their ferociousness be enough against the military might of an empire?

'The djinn owe you a huge debt of gratitude,' he said. 'If ever you need our help, you need only ask, Ramina.'

She smiled and held out her hand, then grasped Emad's forearm, her grip firm but not crushing.

'Thank you, Emad. We will.'

Ramina turned and joined the other manticores. She nodded at Zana.

They'd all said their farewells earlier, before those on guard had opened the doors to the manticores. Emad still blinked back a tear when Zana, about to join his new pride, cast a forlorn glance at a gaunt-looking Yesfir. Behrouz, who avoided looking anyone in the eye since his return from the encampment, waved.

Navid, who'd stood beside the couple, didn't move as Baka's doors closed with a loud *thunk*. Emad watched how the lad didn't move and wondered how long he'd stand like that before he got in someone's way. He wasn't sure if Navid was ready to talk. Anyway, what did one say to a young man who'd lost the twin sister he'd shared every day of his life with?

Words hadn't helped when he'd told Yesfir of Fiqitush's pride in her. They only made her cry more. In time, Emad hoped, Yesfir would draw comfort from those words.

As he'd done with Behrouz, assigning him to lead the defence council in the hope it would rebuild his confidence, Navid needed something to force him out of the room he'd hidden away in. He had an idea, although he couldn't tell if it would work. Emad took a deep breath, straightened his shoulders and strolled over to Navid.

'How are you?' he said.

Navid frowned, although his eyes remained fixed on the doors.

'I miss her,' he said with a thin voice. 'I find myself asking her for an opinion or wanting to point at something I've seen and then, when I open my mouth to speak, I realise she isn't there. I know she's gone, but something inside of me doesn't want to believe it or accept it.'

Emad's throat constricted.

Be strong for the lad's sake.

'I've found the perfect resting place for Roshan's remains,' he said. 'Would you like to see it?'

Navid's head drooped forward. He seemed to Emad to be pondering the question.

'Yes,' he said, then nodded. His eyes narrowed a little. 'That would be good.'

Emad led the way to the ziggurat. They walked together in

silence. Marble of different hues—white, pink and blue—replaced the sandstone walls of the buildings they passed. The djinn had paved the entire city and clad both the battlements and the ziggurat with dark-grey granite. Fiqitush had chosen the materials, having included the designs for new buildings in his tablet's entries.

Emad remembered the djinn cities he'd visited during his time as a sailor. From his recently returned memories, he couldn't remember any of them looking like Baka. He itched to revisit those cities, to learn what had happened to them and discover what became of the other djinn he'd forgotten.

'Your Highness.'

Emad rolled his eyes at the interruption.

Shephatiah climbed the ziggurat's steps two at a time and strode towards them.

'I told you, lad, call me Emad. If you have to use a title, it's Governor. That's what we all agreed, remember? Baka won't be ruled; it will be governed.'

Shephatiah bowed.

'Sorry, Governor Emad.'

Emad wondered if the djinni was always on ceremony and if he ever relaxed.

'Well, what is it? What's so important you almost slipped on one of those polished steps?'

Shephatiah gazed up and nodded to himself.

'Earlier, at dawn, I checked on the two dry wells, like you'd told me to.' His eyes widened and the corners of his mouth rose. 'They're no longer dry.'

The djinni's excitement was infectious.

'That's wonderful,' Emad said, and slapped Shephatiah on the back. No incantation or word of power could redirect water into those wells. Had Baka decided that one well wasn't enough to keep its residents watered? 'Give me an hour. I'll come find you, and you can tell me more.'

Shephatiah looked from Emad to Navid and back to Emad again. His cheeks reddened.

'Oh, I'm sorry.' He bowed. 'I didn't mean to interrupt.'

Before Emad could tell him not to worry, Shephatiah hurried off in the municipal building's direction.

Navid shook his head.

'Ever since you announced I was your son, people look at me that way.'

Emad's palms began to sweat. He canted his head at the ziggurat and started to walk.

'Do you wish I hadn't?'

Navid's brow furrowed.

'I just want everyone to know who Roshan was, that she helped the djinn before we knew who our father was.'

Emad swallowed the lump in his throat. He didn't know how to respond. Thankfully, they'd reached the ziggurat.

'Is this place you've chosen?' Navid said. 'It's in there?'

Emad gestured for them to climb.

As they ascended the stairs, he said, 'The same day Baka rose into the air, a door appeared in the entrance hallway's wall. It leads to a basement.'

A chandelier composed of firestones and resembling an inverted vortex illuminated the windowless hallway. Emad pressed his palm against a wall, then stepped away. A solid sheet of granite swung on silent, invisible hinges.

Firestones flickered on as they descended the stairwell into the basement.

Emad opened his mouth and then closed it. He'd wanted to tell Navid about how he rattled around in the governor's house and its many rooms. Instead of sitting on his own in that single room across from the square, Navid should come and live with him.

Now's not the time. Be patient and just keep an eye on him. If he wants help or company, he'll let you know.

A continuous sheet of lapis lazuli covered the basement's floor. The walls were tiled with coral-red marble, and lights shone from holes in the high ceiling.

'This is how we found it,' Emad said, his voice dampened by the cavernous space surrounding them. 'Everyone who's seen this can't figure out what kind of magic is making light shine from the ceiling.'

Navid turned a full circle. When his gaze met Emad's, his forehead crinkled.

'It's huge...and empty. Where were you thinking of putting the casket?'

Emad expected such a response. When Shephatiah had first shown him the place, he'd wondered what the previous occupants had used it for.

'I want to build a library,' Emad said. He headed for the chamber's centre. 'The seal robbed us of our auric energy and our memories.' He sighed. 'There are only five hundred of us now. Before Solomon arrived, we numbered in the thousands. How much knowledge have we lost? From now on, we must record what we know, preserve it along with the knowledge Fiqitush had kept stored in Iram's library.' He glanced over at Navid. He still hadn't answered the lad's question. 'At the library's centre, there'll be a memorial to Roshan. All of our knowledge will surround her, and she'll also be part of our history. I want the djinn to remember what she did for them.' He paused to allow Navid to think about what he'd said. 'What do you think? If you think Roshan would have preferred something else, I want to hear about it.'

Navid chewed his lip. He folded his arms, then turned to take in his surroundings.

Emad held his hands behind his back to stop himself from fidgeting.

When he faced Emad again, Navid nodded.

'It's a good idea,' he said. 'I think she'd like it.'

Emad grinned and rubbed his sweaty palms on his tunic.

'I do like it.'

Emad swung round, partly out of surprise that someone else was in the basement, but mostly because he recognised the voice.

Roshan stood behind them, close to the foot of the stairs. She pulled back the hood of her robe. Her blue-grey skin lightened to a flesh tone, causing the orange whirls of flame beneath her cheeks and forehead to fade.

She smiled at her brother and then nodded as if to confirm it was her. Roshan looked his way, and Emad's stomach fluttered. He grasped Navid's arm for support.

'Hello, Father,' she said.

27

Sassan hung above a patch of bare ground. Beneath it lay his ashes.

After three sunsets and three sunrises, today would be no different. Alone and ethereal, he'd waited for the Bridge of Judgement to appear, his former life on one side of it and Heaven on the other. He didn't understand how his good deeds and misdeeds would widen or narrow the bridge.

So far, there'd been no bridge to judge him, no tumble from it to start a new cycle of rebirth. He'd died and nothing had happened since. Was God so disappointed in him that this was his punishment, to remain a spectre, left behind and forgotten, not worthy of another chance?

The thought left him furious at being cast aside so casually. Had the Divine Light ignored his years of service and devotion because of one mistake? What kind of god did that?

The air shimmered in front of Sassan. It blurred, then coalesced into a cave lit by the red glow of firestones. A woman sat at a table, an empty chair opposite hers. Her face alternated between a human's and an eagle's.

Sassan recognised the eagle-headed spirit. He also

remembered seeing the woman's face moments before he died. If they were the same, what did that mean?

The head settled on being human. Although her lips didn't move, her voice made his essence vibrate.

'If you wish, you can remain with your ashes, Sassan,' it said. The woman gestured at the empty chair. 'Or you can do the sensible thing and join me, Armaiti, and I will tell you why God has forsaken you.'

A NOTE FROM THE AUTHOR

Thank you for reading this book. This book is part of the first trilogy in the Baka Chronicles. Reader reviews will help me determine whether to keep the series going. Whether it's brief or detailed, your feedback will make a huge difference.

ABOUT THE AUTHOR

J F Mehentee is a British-born Asian with Persian ancestry. A lifelong reader of fantasy and science fiction, he's always looking for ways to combine his interest in Asian and Middle Eastern mythology with storytelling.

After spending three years in Phnom Penh, Cambodia, he now lives in Colombo, Sri Lanka, where he writes full-time—all the while dreaming of one day playing jazz flute like Ron Burgundy.

To learn more, visit www.jfmehentee.com.

ACKNOWLEDGMENTS

Producing the Baka Chronicles has been a team effort. I couldn't have created this series without help from the following professionals:

Structural editor: James Christy,
Copy editor: Richard Shealy,
Cover designer: Deranged Doctor Design.

Finally, huge THANK YOUs to Ginny for her love and encouragement and to my brother, V, who's read just about everything I've ever written—first drafts included!

Published by P in C Publishing

ISBN: 978-1-912402-23-6